Bread

Ed McBain was born in Manhattan, but fled to the Bronx at the age of twelve. He went through elementary and high school in the New York school system, and the Navy claimed him in 1944. When he returned two years later, he attended Hunter College. After a variety of jobs, he worked for a literary agent, where he learnt about plotting stories. When his agent-boss started selling them regularly to magazines, and sold a mystery novel and a juvenile science-fiction title as well, they both decided that it would be more profitable for him to stay at home and write full time.

Under his own name, Evan Hunter, he is the author of a number of novels, including *The Blackboard Jungle*, *Come Winter* and *Every Little Crook and Nanny*. As Ed McBain he has written the highly popular '87th Precinct' series of crime novels, including *Shotgun*, *Jigsaw*, *Fuzz*, *Hail, Hail, the Gang's All Here!* and *Sadie When She Died*, all of which are available in Pan.

Previously published by
Ed McBain in Pan Books

Ed McBain

Bread

An 87th Precinct mystery

Pan Books
London and Sydney

First British edition published 1974 by Hamish Hamilton Ltd
This edition published 1976 by Pan Books Ltd,
Cavaye Place, London SW10 9PG
3rd printing 1978
© Evan Hunter 1974
ISBN 0 330 24850 2
Printed and bound in Great Britain by
Hunt Barnard Printing Ltd, Aylesbury, Bucks

This is for
Yvonne and Jamie Hamilton

The city in these pages is imaginary.
The people, the places are all fictitious.
Only the police routine is based on
established investigatory technique.

1

It was August, and the temperature outside was ninety-six degrees, and the squadroom was not air-conditioned, and Detective Steve Carella was hot. The three rotating electric fans did little more than circulate air that was stale and moist, and there was a hole in one of the window screens (put there by some fun-loving, rock-throwing youngsters) that allowed the entrance of all kinds of flying vermin. A pusher was asleep in the detention cage in one corner of the room, and the phones on two vacant desks were ringing, and Cotton Hawes was talking to his girl friend on another phone at another desk, and Carella's shirt was sticking to his back and he wished he was still on vacation.

This was Wednesday, and he had come back to work on Monday, and half the 87th Squad (or so it seemed) had in turn gone on vacation, and here he was sitting behind a typewriter and a pile of paperwork, a tall, wide-shouldered man who normally looked athletic and lean and somewhat Chinese, what with brown eyes that slanted downward in his face, but who now looked wilted and worn and weary and beleaguered, like a man whose undershorts are slowly creeping up into the crack of his behind, which his were most surely and inexorably doing on this miserable hot day in August.

The man sitting opposite him was named Roger Grimm, no relation to the brothers Jakob and Wilhelm. He looked cool and crisp, albeit agitated, a dumpy little man in his late forties, conservatively dressed in a seersucker suit, pale blue shirt, blue tie of a deeper tint, and white shoes. He was holding a lightweight summer straw in his hands, and he demanded to know where Detective Parker was.

'Detective Parker is on vacation,' Carella said.

'So who's handling my case?' Grimm asked.

'What case is that?' Carella said.

7

'The arson,' Grimm said. 'My warehouse was burned down last week.'

'And Detective Parker was handling the case?'

'Yes, Detective Parker was handling the case.'

'Well, Detective Parker is on vacation.'

'So what am I supposed to do?' Grimm asked. 'I had $500,000 worth of wooden goods in that warehouse. My entire stock was lost in the fire.'

'I'm sorry to hear that,' Carella said, 'but I don't know anything about the case because I just got back from vacation myself. Monday. I got back Monday, and this is Wednesday, and I don't know anything at all about your warehouse.'

'I thought you people worked on cases in pairs,' he said.

'Sometimes we do and sometimes we don't.'

'Well, who was Detective Parker's partner on the case, would you know that?'

'No, but maybe I can find out for you,' Carella said. He turned from his own desk to where Cotton Hawes was sitting not five feet away, still talking on the telephone. 'Cotton,' he said, 'have you got a minute?'

'Okay, Christine, I'll see you at eight,' Hawes said, and then whispered something further into the mouthpiece, and hung up and began walking toward Carella's desk. He was a big man, six-two and weighing a hundred and ninety pounds, with a straight unbroken nose, a good mouth with a wide lower lip, and a square, clefted chin. His red hair was streaked with white over the left temple. He looked very mean this morning of August 14. He wasn't particularly mean, he just looked that way.

'Yeah, Steve?' he said.

'This is Roger Grimm,' Carella said. 'Detective Hawes.'

'How do you do?' Hawes said.

Grimm merely nodded.

'Parker was working on an arson for Mr Grimm, and I've just explained that he's on vacation now, and Mr Grimm was wondering if anybody was on the case with Parker.'

'Yeah,' Hawes said. 'Kling was.'

'Then may I please talk to Kling?' Grimm said.

'He's on vacation,' Hawes said.

'Is the entire Police Department on vacation?' Grimm asked.

'No, *we're* here,' Hawes said.

'Then how about giving me some help?' Grimm said.

'What kind of help do you want?' Carella asked.

'I'm having trouble with the insurance people,' Grimm said. 'I want you to understand that my warehouse was protected with a burglar alarm system hooked into a central station, not to mention two night watchmen and an elaborate sprinkler system on every floor of the building . . .'

'What kind of burglar alarm?' Carella asked, and moved a pad into place and picked up a pencil.

'The best. Very sophisticated. Combination open- and closed-circuit. The arsonist cross-contacted one set of wires and cut the other.'

'How'd he get by your watchmen?' Hawes asked.

'Chloral hydrate. Drugged them both. He also smashed the water main in the basement of the building, so the sprinklers didn't work when the fire got going.'

'Sounds like he knew the layout pretty well.'

'Yes.'

'Got any enemies in the wooden-goods business, Mr Grimm?' Carella asked.

'I have competitors.'

'Did you tell Detective Parker about them?'

'Yes.'

'And?'

'Nothing.'

'What does that mean? Nothing?'

'In Parker's opinion, nobody had a good enough reason for committing a crime that would net him forty years in jail.'

'How about personal enemies? Got any of those?' Hawes asked.

'Everyone has personal enemies,' Grimm said.

'Any who might be capable of something like this?'

'The only one I could think of was a man whose wife I began dating shortly after they were divorced. He's since married

9

again, and he has two children by his new wife. When Parker questioned him, he could barely remember my name.'

'Uh-huh,' Carella said, and nodded. 'What kind of trouble are you having with the insurance company?'

'*Companies*. There's a pair of them involved. $500,000 is a big risk; they shared it between them. Now they've gone to one of these giant adjustment bureaus and asked them to handle the claim. And the bureau told them to hold off settlement until the arsonist is caught or until the Police and Fire Departments are sure *I* didn't set fire to my own damn place.'

'*Did* you set fire to it, Mr Grimm?'

'Of course not,' Grimm said, offended. 'There was $500,000 worth of merchandise in that building. I would have shipped it two days ago . . . that was the twelfth, am I right?'

'Right, Monday the twelfth.'

'Right, I was supposed to ship on the twelfth. So somebody set fire to the warehouse on the seventh, last Wednesday. I usually send out my bills the same day I ship, payable in ten days. If I'd have shipped Monday, when I was supposed to, I'd be getting paid sometime next week, you understand?' Grimm said.

'Not completely,' Carella said. 'You paid $500,000 for the stuff that went up in the fire, is that it?'

'No, I paid about *half* that. Four Deutschemarks for each unit, about a buck and a quarter apiece, including the duty.'

'Then you paid approximately $250,000, is *that* right?'

'That's right. And I insured it for $500,000 because that's what I would have got from my customers ten days after I shipped the stuff. $500,000. That's the fair market value, with firm orders to back it up, and that's what I insured the stock for.'

'So what's the problem?'

'I've got another batch coming from Germany on the twenty-eighth of this month. But I've got nothing to sell now, and if the insurance companies won't reimburse me for my loss, how am I going to pay for the new stuff when it gets here?'

'This new stuff,' Carella said. 'Is it the same as the old stuff?'

'These little wooden animals, right,' Grimm said. 'Four hundred thousand little wooden animals that I'm supposed to pay half a million dollars for, cash on delivery. But if I haven't got the money, how can I pay for the merchandise?'

'Why don't you just cancel the order?' Hawes suggested.

'*Cancel* it?' Grimm asked, appalled. 'I'm into a gold mine here, why would I want to cancel? Look, let me explain this to you, okay? Are you good with figures?'

'I got a ninety in algebra,' Hawes said.

'What?' Grimm said.

'In high school. A ninety in algebra.' Hawes was quite proud of the accomplishment, but Grimm seemed unimpressed. Grimm had money on his mind, and money and mathematics were only distant cousins.

'Here's the history of it,' Grimm said. 'I came into a little cash last year, and was looking for an investment that would give me a good return, you follow? So I happened to be in West Germany just before Christmas, and I spotted these little wooden animals – dogs, cats, rabbits, crap like that, about two inches high, all hand-carved. They were selling for a buck and a quarter each, so I took a gamble, I bought a hundred thousand of them.'

'Cost you $125,000,' Hawes said quickly, still determined to show Grimm that a ninety in algebra was a feat not to be dismissed so easily.

'Right, they cost me $125,000.'

'That's quite a gamble,' Carella said, trying to figure how long it would take him to earn $125,000 on his salary of $14,735 a year.

'Not as it turned out,' Grimm said, smiling with satisfaction. 'I sold them here for $250,000 – doubled my money. And I began getting reorders like crazy. So I took the entire $250,000 and bought *another* batch of little wooden animals.'

'With $250,000 you were able to buy . . .'

'Two hundred thousand of them,' Grimm said.

'Two hundred thousand, right, right,' Hawes said uncertainly.

'And that's what went up in the warehouse fire,' Grimm said.

11

'The problem as I see it,' Hawes said, 'is that you had all these little wooden animals ready to ship . . .'

'Right.'

'For which your customers would have paid you $500,000 . . .'

'Right, right.'

'Which money you would have used to pay for *another* batch coming in on the twenty-eighth of this month.'

'Four hundred thousand of them,' Grimm said.

'Four hundred thousand,' Hawes said. 'That's a lot of little wooden animals.'

'Especially when you realize I can *sell* the little mothers for a *million* dollars.'

'Well, you've certainly got a problem,' Hawes said.

'Which is why I came up here today,' Grimm said. 'To put a little pressure on Parker. *I've* got a desperate situation here, and *he's* sitting on his ass in the sun someplace.'

'What do you want us to do, Mr Grimm?' Carella asked.

'Catch the arsonist. Or at least vouch for me. Tell the adjustment bureau I'm clean, I had nothing to do with the fire.'

'I don't know any police officer in his right mind who'd do that, Mr Grimm. Too many people *do* set fire to their own businesses. Your stock was insured for $500,000. That's a lot of money. I'm sure Detective Parker was considering the possibility that you did the job yourself.'

'Why would I? I had firm orders for the entire stock. It was waiting to be *shipped*!'

'I'm merely trying to explain why Detective Parker wouldn't go out on a limb.'

'So what am I supposed to do?' Grimm asked, and wet his lips and looked suddenly thoughtful. 'How long will Parker be gone?'

'Two weeks.'

'And his partner, whatever his name is?'

'Kling. Two weeks also.'

'That's impossible. Look, you've got to help me.'

'We're helping you, Mr Grimm,' Carella said.

'We're helping you,' Hawes echoed.

Grimm looked at them skeptically. 'I know if I put a little

pressure on the insurance companies, they'll pay me in three, four weeks, maybe a month the latest. But that's not soon enough. I need the money in fourteen days, when the boat gets here from West Germany. Otherwise they won't release the cargo, and I'm up the creek. You've got to catch this guy before my shipment arrives.'

'Well, it's Parker's case,' Carella said.

'So what? Don't you ever help each other out on cases?'.

'Sometimes. But usually, we've got our own case loads, and we ...'

'This is unusual,' Grimm said, and then repeated it, as though the detectives had not heard him the first time. 'This is unusual. There's a time element involved here. I've got to get that insurance money before the boat gets here. Can't you help me? Are you so damn busy up here that you can't give a little help to an honest citizen who's been *victimized*, and who's trying to get back on his feet again? Is that too much to ask of the Police Department?'

'You don't understand the way it works,' Hawes said.

'I don't *care* how it works. You're supposed to protect the *innocent*, too, you know. Instead of running around the streets busting teen-agers for smoking pot, why don't you earn your salaries?'

'I haven't busted a teen-ager in at least two hours,' Hawes said dryly.

'All right, all right, I'm sorry,' Grimm said. 'I know you guys work hard, I know you've got to have some sort of organization up here, or the job would get overwhelming. I realize that. But I'm begging you to please help me with this. Bend the rules a little, take Parker's case while he's away. Help me find the son of a bitch who burned down my place. I'd go to a private detective, but I simply haven't got the money. Please. Will you please help me?'

'We'll see what we can do,' Carella said. 'We'll check the files, see what Parker's got on it. If there's anything we can follow up, we will.'

'Thank you,' Grimm said. 'Thank you very, very much.' He reached into his wallet. 'Here's my card,' he said. 'Office number and home number. Please call me if you need any more information. And, of course, if you come up with something...'

'We'll let you know,' Carella said.

'Thank you,' Grimm said again, and put on his straw hat and went out through the gate in the slatted wooden railing that separated the squadroom from the corridor outside.

Both men waited until they were sure he was out of earshot. Then Hawes said, 'Are you really going to pick this up for Parker?'

'Well, I'll take a look at what he's got on it, anyway.'

'Far as I'm concerned,' Hawes said, 'Parker can handle his own damn cases.'

'Yeah, well,' Carella said, and shrugged.

Hawes looked up at the clock. 'You mind if I leave a little early?' he asked. 'I've got a date tonight.'

'No, go ahead,' Carella said. He, too, looked up at the clock. 'Meyer and Brown ought to be relieving soon, anyway.'

'See you tomorrow, then,' Hawes said.

'Right.'

Hawes pulled up his tie, put on his jacket, and left the squadroom. Carella glanced at his scribbled notes, rolled a sheet of paper into the typewriter, and began typing:

	NUMBER OF LITTLE WOODEN ANIMALS	COST AT $1.25 EACH	RESALE VALUE AT $2.50 EACH
Order #1	100,000	$125,000	$250,000 (which Grimm then reinvested)
Order #2	200,000 (which were lost in fire)	$250,000	$500,000 (which Grimm needs to pay for cargo arriving 8/28)
Order #3	400,000 (arriving 8/28)	$500,000 (which Grimm will not have unless insurance people pay up)	$1,000,000

It was always clarifying to see things in chart form.

Grimm had come into a little cash last year ($125,000 wasn't exactly a *little* cash in Carella's neighborhood, and Carella wondered precisely *how* Grimm had come into it) and had invested the money in little wooden animals which he had resold here for $250,000. He had then reinvested in a *second* wooden menagerie for which he had firm orders totaling $500,000. He had planned to use this money to pay for a *third* shipment of miniature beasts on the twenty-eighth of the month, reselling them in turn and making himself a millionaire. That was nice work if you could get it. But there are spoilsports everywhere, and apparently someone was determined to see that Grimm *didn't* get it.

A million dollars, Carella thought. For buying and selling little wooden animals. When he got home tonight, he would tell his nine-year-old son Mark that there was no percentage in the crime biz, not on the cop side of it and certainly not on the crook side of it. The thing to get into, he would say, is little wooden animals. That's where the future lies, son. Little wooden animals. And April, Mark's twin sister, would listen wide-eyed, wondering whether Carella was joking, and wondering why *she* had not been advised to undertake a similar professional pursuit. Was it possible her father was a male chauvinist pig? (Or as she was wont to pronounce it, after having heard the expression on television, 'a male show-business pig.') Teddy, the mother of his children, his wife, would listen by watching, her eyes never leaving his lips, a secret, silent, amused expression on her face. And then perhaps she would answer with her hands, using the deaf-mute language her entire family understood, and she would tell the children that their father was joking, the future was *not* in little wooden animals, it was instead in compressed garbage, which she had read could be made virtually indestructible after treatment with radioactive isotopes, and could then be sawed, planed, molded, hammered, and used for all sorts of things. The only problem was how to get rid of the indestructible things made from this specially treated waste. Garbage, she would tell them. Wooden animals, he would insist.

Smiling, he went to the files.

*

Cotton Hawes, who was a bachelor, had no children (that he knew of) to advise on future career possibilities. His *own* father, who had proudly named him after Cotton Mather, the Puritan priest, had once told Hawes that the only god worth serving was God Himself. Hawes had pondered this for a long time. He had pondered it all through adolescence, when the only god worth serving seemed to be hidden somewhere beneath the skirts of every high school girl who wandered tantalizingly into his field of vision. He had pondered it during his hitch in the Navy, when the only god worth serving seemed to be survival, a not always certain prospect aboard a PT boat. And he had pondered it when he joined the police force, where the god was justice (he thought at first) and where the god later became retribution (until he learned otherwise) and where the god after his transfer to the 87th seemed embodied in the person of Steve Carella (who he later learned was only a mere mortal, like himself). He was no longer a boy listening to his father, a good and decent man (although a bit of a fanatic when it came to religion), advising him on how to live his life. He had, in fact, needed no better advice than the example his father had set simply by being what he was. Hawes tried to be a good and decent man. He didn't know whether he was or not, but that's what he tried to be.

He did not get back from his evening and night with Christine Maxwell, whom he had met many years ago while investigating a multiple murder in a bookshop, until three AM. He called his answering service, and learned that Steve Carella had phoned while he was out and left a message for him to return the call no matter what time it was. He immediately dialed Carella's home in Riverhead.

'Hello?' Carella said. His voice was edged with sleep.

'Steve, this is Cotton. I'm sorry I woke you, but your message said . . .'

'Yeah, that's all right,' Carella said. He was coming awake.

He paused for a moment, and then said, 'Roger Grimm called the squadroom at a little past midnight. Meyer took the call.'

'What's up?' Hawes asked.

'While he was out tonight, somebody burned his house to the ground. I'm going over to take a look at the warehouse tomorrow. How'd you like to drive up to Logan and see what they did to his house?'

'Sure thing, Steve. What time do you want me there?'

'Ten o'clock too early?'

'No, no, fine,' Hawes said, and looked at the clock and sighed.

2

On the drive out to the suburb of Logan the next morning, it occurred to Hawes that Roger Grimm might have set fire to his own house, in order to collect the insurance money on it, in order to obtain some ready cash, in order to release at least part of the cargo of wooden doo-dads he was expecting from Germany. He arrived in Logan at ten-fifteen, and one look at the house, even in its gutted condition, convinced him that insurance fraud was a definite possibility. Set on a half-acre of rolling ground in an area of luxurious estates, the house alone must have been worth at least a quarter of a million dollars before the fire.

In its present condition, it was worth zilch. Whoever had set the blaze had done an expert job. Even though the Fire Department had responded within minutes, the house was almost totally consumed by the time they got there, and they'd been more concerned with rescuing the rest of the neighborhood than they'd been with salvaging Grimm's house. In a particularly dry August, they had not wanted an uncontrollable conflagration on their hands. They'd done a good job wetting down rooftops and shrubbery, containing the blaze, so that the only thing reduced to ashes was Grimm's place.

Hawes parked his convertible Pontiac, and then walked up the oval driveway to the still-smoldering ruin. Grimm was standing on the flagstone entry porch before the charred posts and lintel of what had once been the front door. He was wearing white slacks and a dark blue, short-sleeved sports shirt. His hands were in his back pockets, and he was staring through the doorless frame as though hoping to find some semblance of a house beyond it. He heard Hawes's approach and turned suddenly. There was a pained and distant look on his face.

'Oh, hello,' he said.

'Was it insured?' Hawes asked.

'What? Oh. Yes. Yes, it was insured.'

'For how much?'

'Three hundred thousand.' He turned to look at the rubble again. 'I put a lot of work into this place,' he said. 'This isn't like the warehouse. The warehouse was only money, a lot of wooden crap that represented money. This is different. This was where I lived.'

'When did it happen?'

'Fire Department clocked the call at eleven-twenty.'

'Who phoned them?'

'The man next door. He was getting ready for bed and he looked out from an upstairs window and saw the flames. He called the Fire Department right away.'

'What's his name?'

'George Aronowitz.'

'Well, let's take a look around,' Hawes said.

'No,' Grimm said, and shook his head. 'No, I don't want to. I'll wait for you here.'

A burglarized apartment is a violation of self, and there is nothing quite so pathetic as the look on the face of a burglary victim. He stands in the midst of an invasion of privacy, clothing scattered, personal belongings treated with indignity and haste, and he is reduced to helpless rage and child-like dependency. A sense of vulnerability, frailty, even, yes, mortality bounces from the walls of his invaded castle, and he feels in that moment that he himself, his *person*, is no longer safe from the wanton, willful violation of total strangers. Murder, of course, is the ultimate theft. It robs a man not only of his possessions but of his very life. Arson runs a close second.

There is undisputed excitement in watching a roaring blaze, perhaps a throwback to those days when Neanderthal struck flint against tinder and leaped back in surprise at what he had miraculously wrought. Or perhaps it is something deeper, something evil and dark that causes man to respond to a fire raging uncontrolled, something that echoes his own inner desire for the same sort of violent, irrepressible freedom – oh, to be able to challenge and defy, to roar rebellion and command complete and awed attention, to terrorize spectacularly, to rule with undisputed power, and finally to triumph! It's not surprising that some firebugs will watch their handiwork in total ecstasy, erections bulging in their trousers, ejaculations dampening their own hot passions when hoses fail to quench the rampaging flames. There is excitement in a fire, and the naked ape responds generically. There is no excitement in the aftermath. A fireman does not fight a fire, he fights the *thing* that is on fire. He drenches it with water, he sprays it with carbon dioxide, he hacks at it with an ax, he does all he can to destroy the *thing* because the fire is only a parasite feasting on the thing, and if he can kill the thing, he can kill the fire. There were a lot of dead things in the rubble of Roger Grimm's home. They lay in sodden steaming chaos like dismembered corpses on a battlefield, partial reminders of what they must have been when they possessed lives of their own.

Like an archaeologist mentally reconstructing an earthen jug from the handle or the lip, Hawes picked gingerly through the ruins, finding charred, blistered, and melted remnants of what had once been a sofa, a record player, a toothbrush, a martini pitcher. There had not been a living soul in the house during the fire, only things that once had lived and now were dead. He could understand why Grimm had no stomach for wading through this inanimate carnage. He searched diligently for some trace of the device that had started the blaze, but found nothing. Alerted to the likelihood of arson, the Logan police would undoubtedly make their own thorough search and perhaps find more than he had. Hawes doubted it. He went outside, talked briefly with Grimm, told him they'd be in touch, and then went next door to the Aronowitz house.

The maid informed Hawes that Mr Aronowitz had left for work at nine that morning and could be reached at his office in the city. She gave Hawes his business number and suggested that he call Mr Aronowitz there. She would not reveal the name or address of the firm for which he worked. Hawes got into his car, drove to the nearest phone booth, and dialed the number the maid had given him. The answering voice said, 'Blake, Fields and Henderson, good morning.'

'Good morning', Hawes said. 'George Aronowitz, please.'

'Moment', the voice said.

Hawes waited. Another voice came onto the line.

'Art Department.'

'Mr Aronowitz, please.'

'Busy, can you hold?'

Hawes held.

'Ringing now,' the voice said, and a third voice came onto the line almost immediately.

'Mr Aronowitz's office.'

'May I speak to him, please?' Hawes said.

'May I ask who's calling?'

'Detective Hawes, 87th Squad.'

'Yes, sir, just a moment.'

Hawes waited.

George Aronowitz was in the middle of a sentence when he finally came onto the line. '. . . want those chromos back by twelve noon or his ass'll be in a sling. You tell him that exactly,' he said. 'Yes, hello?'

'Mr Aronowitz?'

'Yes?'

'This is Detective Hawes, I'm investigating the Grimm fire, and I wonder if you can spare a few minutes . . .'

'Yes?' he said.

'May I stop by to see you sometime today?'

'Can't we do this over the phone?'

'I'd rather talk to you personally.'

'Who did you say you were?'

'Detective Hawes.'

'Who are you with? The Logan police?'

'No, I'm with the 87th Squad. Right here in the city.'

'Hell of a thing, wasn't it?' Aronowitz said. 'Burned right down to the ground. Let me look at my schedule. What'd you say your name was?'

'Detective Hawes.'

'Detective *Horse*?'

'*Hawes*. H-a-w-e-s.'

'How soon can you get here? I've got a lunch date at twelve-thirty.'

'Where are you?'

'Nine-three-three Wilson. Fourteenth floor.'

'I'm in Logan now, give me forty minutes,' Hawes said.

'See you,' Aronowitz said, and hung up.

*

Detective Andy Parker was sitting in his undershorts drinking a bottle of beer in the kitchen of his apartment, and he was supposed to be on vacation, and he was not very happy to see Steve Carella. Carella, who was *never* very happy to see Parker, even under the best of circumstances, did not particularly enjoy seeing him now, in his undershorts. Parker looked like a slob even when he was fully dressed. In his undershorts, sitting at the enamel-topped table and scratching his balls with one hand while tilting the bottle of beer to his lips with the other, he hardly seemed a candidate for *Gentlemen's Quarterly*. His hair was uncombed, and he had not shaved since last Saturday when his vacation had started, and this was Thursday, and from the smell of him, he had not bothered to bathe, either.

Carella did not like Parker.

Parker did not like Carella.

Carella thought Parker was a lazy cop and a bad cop and the kind of cop who gave other cops a bad name. Parker thought Carella was an eager cop and a Goody Two-Shoes cop and the kind of cop who gave other cops a bad name. Only once in Parker's life had he admitted to himself that perhaps Carella was the kind of cop he himself might have become, the kind of cop he perhaps even longed to be, and that was when a body had turned up bearing Carella's identification and it was presumed Carella was dead. Drunk in bed with a whore that night, Parker had buried his head in the pillow and mumbled, 'He was a good cop.' But that had been a long time ago, and Carella had been alive all along, and here he was now, bugging Parker about a goddamn arson case when he was supposed to be on vacation.

'I don't see why this can't wait till I get back,' he said. 'What's the big rush here? This guy married to the mayor's daughter or something?'

'No, just an ordinary citizen,' Carella said.

'Yeah, so ordinary citizens are getting hit on the head every day of the week in this city, and we handle *those* cases in our own sweet time, and some we crack and some we don't. *This* guy loses a bunch of wooden crap in a fire, and he gets hysterical.' Parker belched and immediately swallowed another mouthful of beer. He had not yet offered Carella a bottle, but Carella was already prepared with a brilliant squelch if and when Parker decided to extend at least a small measure of hospitality to a hard-working colleague.

'Grimm feels he's been victimized,' Carella said.

'Everybody in this city is victimized one way or another every day of the week. What makes Grimm so special? I'm supposed to be on vacation. Doesn't Grimm ever take vacations?'

'Andy,' Carella said, 'I came over here only because I couldn't get you on the phone . . .'

'That's right, it's off the hook. I'm on vacation.'

'And I can't find the file on this case. If you'll tell me . . .'

'That's right, there *ain't* no file,' Parker said. 'I was only *on* the case a lousy two days, you know. I caught the squeal late Wednesday night, I worked the case all day Thursday and Friday, and then I started my vacation. How could there be a file on it?'

'Didn't you type up any reports?'

'I didn't have time to type up reports, I was too busy out in the field. Look, Steve, I busted my ass on this case, and I don't need you telling me I was dogging it. I went over that warehouse with a fine-tooth comb,' Parker said, gathering steam. 'I couldn't find a thing, no fuse, no wick, no mechanical device, no bottles that might've had chemicals in them, nothing. I talked to . . .'

'Is it possible the fire was accidental?'

'How could it be? The two watchmen were doped, which means somebody wanted them out of the way, right? Okay, so why? To set fire to the joint.'

'You think Grimm might've done it himself?'

'Not a chance. All the stock was committed, he was ready to ship the stuff the next Monday morning. There were no records or books in the warehouse, he keeps those in an office on Bailey Street. So why would he burn down the joint? He's clean.'

'Then why wouldn't you tell that to his insurers?'

'Because I wasn't sure. I only worked the case two days, and all I had at the end of that time was a pile of ashes. You think I was going to stick my neck out for Grimm? Screw that noise, buddy.'

'Did you get anything from the night watchmen?' Carella asked.

'They're two old farts,' Parker said, 'they can hardly remember their own names. They both got to work at eight o'clock, they remember feeling dizzy about ten, and then blooie. One of them collapsed in the courtyard outside. The other guy was inside making his rounds when it hit him. The firemen thought it was smoke inhalation at first, but that didn't explain why the *outside* man was unconscious. Also, he had his head in a pool of his own vomit, so somebody got the bright idea he'd been doped. They pumped him out at the hospital, and sure enough, he'd been given a healthy dose of chloral hydrate. Okay, so where does that leave me? Chloral hydrate ain't called "knock-out drops" for nothing, the stuff works in minutes. But both watchmen got to the warehouse at eight, and they didn't pass out till two hours later. They told me nobody came anywhere near the place during that time, but *nobody*. So who gave them the knockout drops? You're so hot to crack this one, find the guy who slipped them the Mickey. He's probably the same guy who burned down the joint.'

'You mind if I talk to those watchmen again?' Carella asked.

'Be my guest,' Parker said. 'I'm on vacation. I done all I could before I left, and I don't intend to do anything else till I get back.' He rose, walked to the wall telephone, ripped a piece of paper from the pad beneath it, and began scribbling on it. 'Here're their names,' he said. 'Have fun.'

'Thanks,' Carella said, and got up, and started for the door.

Belatedly and reluctantly, Parker said, 'While you're here, you want a bottle of beer?'

'I'm not allowed to drink on duty,' Carella said, and walked out.

*

The Art Department of Blake, Fields and Henderson occupied the entire fourteenth floor of 933 Wilson Avenue. George Aronowitz was a short, stubby man in his early forties, totally bald, with a walrus mustache that compensated for the lack of hair on his head. His office was starkly decorated in white – white walls, white furniture, white lighting fixtures – the better to exhibit the various posters, magazine ads, photographs, and bits and pieces of artwork he'd either done himself, commissioned, or admired. All of these were tacked to the walls with push-pins, so that he resembled a stout deity sitting in a stained-glass window or a mosaic niche. He shook Hawes's hand briefly, folded his stubby fingers across his chest, leaned back in his swivel chair, and said, 'Shoot.'

'I want to know all about the fire last night.'

'I saw the flames at a little after eleven. I called the Fire Department and they came right over.' Aronowitz shrugged. 'That's about it.'

'Hear anything before that?'

'Like what?'

'Any unusual sounds outside? Dog barking, car driving in, ashcan being knocked over, glass breaking? Anything out of the ordinary?'

'Let me think,' Aronowitz said. 'There're always dogs barking in that neighborhood, so that wouldn't have been out of the ordinary. Everybody *around* there keeps a dog. I hate dogs. Rotten, filthy animals, bite you on the ass for no reason at all.'

'I take it you don't keep a dog.'

'I wouldn't keep a dog if it could talk six languages and read and write Sanskrit. I hate dogs. Grimm doesn't have a dog, either.'

'Well, *were* there dogs barking last night?'

'There are *always* dogs barking,' Aronowitz said. 'Damn things won't shut up. One of them barks at a moth or something, and next thing you know, some other hound is yapping at him from over the hill, and *he* gets answered by *another* stupid mutt, and they keep going all night long, barking at nothing. It's a miracle anybody gets any sleep around there. And it's supposed to be an exclusive neighborhood! If I had my way, I'd poison every dog in the United States of America. Then I'd have them stuffed and put on wheels, and anybody who's a dog lover could buy himself a stuffed one and wheel him around the house, and he wouldn't bark all night long. God, I hate dogs!'

'Did you, ah, hear anything besides dogs barking last night?'

'Who can hear anything with all those mutts howling?' Aronowitz asked. He was becoming very agitated.

Hawes thought he had best change the subject before Aronowitz began frothing at the mouth. 'Let's try to work out a timetable, okay? Maybe that'll help us.'

'What do you mean?'

'Well, for example, what time did you get home last night?'

'Six-thirty,' Aronowitz said.

'Did you pass the Grimm house?'

'Sure. He's right next door, I pass the house every day.'

'Everything seem all right at that time?'

'Everything seemed fine.'

'Nobody lurking around or anything?'

'Nobody. Well, wait a minute, the gardener was watering the lawn at the Franklin house across the way. But he's their regular gardener, he's there maybe three, four times a week. I wouldn't consider that lurking, would you? You should see the dog *they've* got, a big Great Dane who comes bounding out of the driveway like a lion, he could tear out your throat in one gulp. God, what a monster!'

'What'd you do then? After you got home?'

'I changed my clothes, and I had a couple of martinis before dinner.'

'Are you married, Mr Aronowitz?'

'Fourteen years to the same woman. She hates dogs, too.'

'Did *she* hear anything unusual last night?'

'No. At least, she didn't mention anything.'

'Okay, you had dinner at ... what time?'

26

'About seven-thirty, eight o'clock.'

'Then what?'

'We went outside and sat on the terrace, and had some brandy and listened to some music.'

'Until what time?'

'Ten o'clock.'

'No strange sounds outside?'

'None.'

'What'd you do then?'

'Well,' Aronowitz said, and shrugged.

'Yes?'

'Well . . . this is sort of personal.' He hesitated, looked down at his folded hands, and shyly said, 'We made love.'

'Okay,' Hawes said.

'We didn't hear anything while we were making love,' Aronowitz said.

'Okay,' Hawes said.

'Afterwards, we went upstairs. I was getting ready for bed when I happened to look out the window. Grimm's lights were still on, and the place was in flames.'

'In other words, between the time you got home and the time you went upstairs to bed, nothing unusual happened.'

'Well, yes,' Aronowitz said.

'What?' Hawes said, leaning forward.

'We made love on the terrace. That's unusual. We usually do it upstairs in the bedroom.'

'Yes, but aside from that . . .'

'Nothing.'

'Mr Aronowitz, did you happen to glance over at the Grimm house any time *before* you noticed the fire?'

'I guess so. We were on the terrace, and the terrace faces Grimm's house, so I guess we looked at it occasionally. Why?'

'This was after dinner, am I correct? You were on the terrace until about ten o'clock . . .'

'Well, even later,' Aronowitz said. 'We were listening to *music* until ten o'clock, but after that . . .'

'Yes, I understand. What I'm trying to find out is whether there were any lights showing in the Grimm house?'

27

'Lights? You mean . . .'

'At any time during the night, did you notice lights in the Grimm house?'

'Well . . . no. I guess not. I think the house was dark.'

'But the lights *were* on when you noticed the fire.'

'Yes,' Aronowitz said, and frowned.

'Thank you,' Hawes said.

'I don't get it,' Aronowitz said. 'Why would anybody turn on the lights if he was about to set a fire?'

3

Except in cases of pyromania, where the perpetrator acts without conscious motive, there are very real reasons for arson, and every cop in the world knows them by heart.

Parker had checked out Grimm's competitors in the brisk wooden-goods trade, and expressed the opinion that none of them had sufficient motive for committing a crime as heavy as arson. Well, even if Carella respected Parker's judgment (which he didn't), he'd have been unwilling to accept such a sweeping acquittal. Competition was possibly the *strongest* motive for arson, and Carella wasn't about to dismiss Grimm's business rivals as suspects until he'd checked them out thoroughly himself. Nor was he willing to dismiss insurance fraud (First Comic: 'Hello, Sam, I hear you had a big fire in your store last night. Second Comic: 'Shhh, that's *tomorrow* night!') or the destruction of books and records as alternate motives, even though Parker seemed convinced that Grimm was clean. As for extortion, intimidation, or revenge, those possibilities would also depend on what they could learn about Mr Roger Grimm. For all Carella knew, Grimm may have been hobnobbing with all sorts of criminal types who'd finally decided to make things hot for him. Or maybe there were a dozen people Grimm had screwed in the past, all of whom might have been capable of setting the torch to his house, his warehouse, and also the brim of his straw hat. Carella would have to wait and see.

The remaining possible motive was that someone had set the warehouse fire in order to conceal a crime. (Have you left jimmy marks on the windows and fingerprints all over the wall safe? So what? Just burn down the joint as you're leaving.) Curious reasoning, admittedly, since Burglary/One was punishable by a maximum of thirty and a minimum of ten, whereas Arsons/One, Two, and Three were punishable respectively by forty, twenty-five, and fifteen – but who can fathom the intri-

29

cate workings of the criminal mind? And whereas the warehouse fire had probably succeeded in obliterating any evidence of theft, it was highly improbable that anyone would steal an indeterminate amount of wooden animals and then set fire to the remainder of the stock to conceal such petty pilfering. Moreover, if someone *had* committed a crime at the warehouse and then committed arson to *conceal* the crime, it was ridiculous to believe he would later burn down Grimm's house as a cover for the *initial* cover. Such an elaborate smoke screen was for the comic books.

Which left pyromania.

When Carella first learned about the warehouse fire, he'd thought it might have been set by a firebug, despite the fact that two night watchmen had been drugged – pyromaniacs will rarely go to such limits. But the minute he learned of the *second* fire, Carella knew for certain they were not dealing with a nut. In all his experience with pyromaniacs, he had never met a single one with any real motive for setting a fire. Most of them had done it for kicks, not always but often sexually oriented. They liked to watch the flames, they liked to hear the fire engines, they liked the excitement of the crowds, they liked the tumult and the frenzy. They ranged in age from ten to a hundred and ten, they were usually loners, male or female, intellectual or half-wit, corporation executive or short-order cook. Two of the pyros he'd arrested were male alcoholics. Another was a hysterical, pregnant woman. Still another said she'd set a fire only because she was suffering menstrual cramps. All of them had picked their fire sites at random, usually because the building looked 'safe' – vacant, abandoned, or in a lonely, unpatrolled neighborhood.

Most firebugs were very sad people. Carella had known only one funny firebug during all his years as a cop, and he supposed *that* one couldn't have been considered a true pyromaniac at all. He was, in fact, a man Carella had locked up for Armed Robbery. When the man was released from Castleview, he called Carella at the squadroom and told him to come over to his place right away, without his gun, or else he was going to set fire to his own kid brother. His kid brother happened to be thirty-six years old, a man who himself had been in and out of jail since the time he was fifteen. His barbecue, if carried out as threatened, would have caused very little grief up at the old squadroom. So Carella told his Castleview friend to go ahead and set fire to his brother, and hung up. Naturally, the man didn't do it. But there were many nuts in the city for which Carella worked, and not *all* of them were in the Police Department, and he was sure that *none* of them had set Grimm's fires.

Grimm's warehouse was on Clinton Street and Avenue L, adjacent to the waterfront docks on the River Harb. The building was made of red brick, four stories high, with a padlocked cyclone fence running completely around it. A man in his sixties, wearing a watchman's uniform, pistol holstered at his side, was standing inside the gate as Carella pulled up in his Chevy sedan. Carella showed him his police shield, and the man took a key from a ring on his belt and unlocked the gate for him.

'You with the 87th Squad?' he asked.

'Yes,' Carella said.

'Because they've already been here, you know.'

'Yes, I know that,' Carella said. 'I'm Detective Carella, who are you?'

'Frank Reardon,' he said.

'Do you know the men who were on duty the night of the fire, Mr Reardon?'

'Yep. Jim Lockhart and Lenny Barnes. I know them.'

'Have you seen them since?'

'See them every night. They relieve me every night at eight o'clock on the dot.'

'They mention anything about what happened?'

'Only that somebody doped them up. What'd you want to look at first, Mr Carella?'

'The basement.'

Reardon locked the gate behind them, and then led Carella across a cobblestoned courtyard to a metal fire door on the side of the building. He unlocked the door with a key from the ring on his belt, and they went inside. After the bright sunlight outdoors, the small hallway they entered seemed much dimmer than it really was. Carella followed Reardon down a dark flight of stairs that terminated abruptly in a basement still flooded with water from the broken main. Half a dozen drowned rats were floating near the furnace. The shattered pipe was one of those huge, near-indestructible cast-iron jobs. It seemed evident to Carella that the arsonist had used an explosive charge on it. It also seemed evident that he had not set his fire in the basement of the building, it being difficult for fires to burn underwater.

'Want to take a little swim?' Reardon asked, and cackled unexpectedly.

'Let's take a look upstairs, okay?'

'Nothing to see up there,' Reardon said. 'Fire done a pretty good job.'

The fire had indeed done a pretty good job, nor was it difficult to understand how $500,000 worth of miniature wooden rabbits, puppy dogs, and pussy cats had provided excellent tinder for a blaze of monumental proportions. The mess underfoot was a combination of water-logged ashes and charcoal, with here and there a recognizable head, tail, or paw. The crates had probably been piled on metal tables, the scorched and twisted remnants of which had been shoved aside or thrown over by the firemen in their efforts to quench the flames. Hanging light fixtures with metal shades, their bulbs shattered by the heat, were spaced evenly across the high ceiling of the room. One of these fixtures caught Carella's attention because a fire-frayed length of electrical wire was dangling from its bulb socket. He pulled a table over and climbed onto it. The length of wire was an extension cord equipped with a fitting that screwed into the socket ordinarily occupied by the bulb. The hanging wire had been burned short by the fire, but it was reasonable to assume it had once been long enough to reach from the fixture down to one of the tables.

Carella frowned.

He frowned because Andy Parker was supposed to be a cop, and cops are supposed to know that most criminal fires are not started with matches; since the whole idea of arson is to be far away from the place when it bursts into flame, such instant ignition is impractical and dangerous. Parker had mentioned that he'd conducted a thorough search for wicks, fuses, mechanical devices, traces of chemicals – anything that would have caused delayed ignition. But he had not noticed the hanging extension cord, and the only thing Carella could assume was that Parker had been too intent on his vacation to spot what could easily have been a primitive but highly effective incendiary device. He had investigated too many arsons in the past (and he was sure Parker had as well) where the fires had been started by wrapping an electric light bulb in wool, rayon, or chiffon, and then suspending it over a pile of highly inflammable material such as movie film, cotton, excelsior, or simple wood shavings.

With Reardon at his elbow, Carella, still frowning, walked across the room to the light switch near the entrance door. The toggle was in the ON position. This meant that the arsonist, working with a flashlight in the dark, could have screwed in his extension cord, hung his light bulb over the prepared nest of combustibles, walked to the door, turned on the light switch, and left the building – secure that he'd have a merry conflagration in a short period of time.

'Anybody dust this light switch?' he asked Reardon.

'What?'

'Did any of the lab technicians examine this switch for fingerprints?'

'Gee, I don't know,' Reardon said. 'Why?'

Carella reached into his inside jacket pocket and pulled out a sheaf of evidence tags. From his side pocket, and musing on the fact that a cop in the field is a walking stationery store, he removed a small roll of Scotch tape. He yanked one of the evidence tags from under the rubber band holding the stack together and then Scotch-taped it, top and bottom, over the light switch. 'Somebody'll be here later,' he told Reardon. 'Leave this just the way it is.'

'Okay,' Reardon said. He looked puzzled.

'Mind if I use your phone?'

'On the wall outside,' Reardon said. 'Near the clock.'

Carella went out into the corridor. Scribbled onto the wall

in pencil alongside the phone were the names and numbers of Reardon's counterparts, Lockhart and Barnes. Carella dialed the Police Laboratory downtown on High Street and spoke to a lab assistant named Jeff Warren, telling him what he thought and requesting that somebody come to the warehouse to dust the switch. Warren told him they were up to their asses at the moment with a pile of dirty clothes from a suspected murderer's apartment, going through it all for laundry and dry-cleaning marks, and he doubted anybody could get up there before morning. Carella told him to do the best he could, hung up, and fished in his pocket for another dime. He found only three quarters, and asked Reardon if he had any change. Reardon gave him two dimes and a nickel, and Carella dialed Lockhart's number from the penciled scrawl on the warehouse wall.

Lockhart sounded sleepy when he answered the phone. Carella belatedly remembered that he was dealing with a night watchman and instantly apologized for having awakened him. Lockhart said he hadn't been asleep and asked what Carella wanted. Carella told him he was investigating the Grimm fire and would appreciate talking to him and Barnes if the three of them could get together sometime later in the afternoon. They agreed on three o'clock, and Lockhart said he would call Barnes to tell him about the meeting. Carella thanked him and hung up. Reardon was still at his elbow.

'Yes?' Carella said.

'They won't be able to tell you anything,' Reardon said. 'The other cop already talked to them.'

'Have any idea what they said?'

'Me? How would I know?'

'I thought they were friends of yours.'

'Well, they relieve me every night, but that's about it.'

'What've you got here?' Carella asked. 'Three shifts?'

'Just two,' Reardon said. 'Eight in the morning till eight at night, and vice versa.'

'Those are long shifts,' Carella said.

Reardon shrugged. 'It ain't a hard job,' he said. 'And most of the time, nothing happens.'

※

Carella treated himself to a long, leisurely lunch at a French restaurant on Meredith Street, wishing that his wife were there to share the meal with him. There is perhaps nothing more lonely than eating a French meal all by yourself, unless it's eating Chinese food alone, but then the Chinese are experts at torture. Carella rarely longed for Teddy's company while coping with the minute-by-minute aggravations of police work, but here and now, relieved of routine for just a little while, he wished she were there to talk to him.

Contrary to the opinion of some male show-business pigs who surmised that being married to a beautiful deaf-mute guaranteed a lifetime of submissive silence, Teddy was the most talkative woman Carella knew. She talked with her face, she talked with her hands, she talked with her eyes, she even 'talked' when *he* was talking, her lips unconsciously mouthing the words his own lips formed as she watched and read the words. They talked together about everything and anything. He suspected that the day they stopped talking would be the day they stopped loving each other. Even their fights (and her silent raging anger was frightening to behold, those eyes flashing, those fingers shooting sparks of molten fury) were a form of talking, and he cherished them as he cherished Teddy herself. He ate his Duck Bigarade in silence, alone, and then drove to Stiller Avenue for his three o'clock appointment with Lockhart and Barnes.

Clearview, in Calm's Point, was a section of the city variously labeled 'heterogeneous,' 'fragmented,' or 'alienated,' depending on who was doing the labeling. Carella saw it for exactly what it was: a festering slum in which white men, black men, and Puerto Ricans lived elbows-to-buttocks in abject poverty. Perhaps Mr Agnew, who had seen one slum and therefore seen them all, had never had to work in one. Carella worked in a great many different slums as part of his everyday routine, and since he was not a milkman or a letter carrier or a Bible salesman, but was instead a police officer, his job sometimes got a bit difficult. If there is one thing the residents of a slum can detect immediately, it is the smell of a cop. Slum dwellers do not like policemen. Being a cop (and naturally being a bit defensive about judgments made on the basis of whether or not a man is carrying a police shield), Carella could nonetheless recognize the fact that slum dwellers, both criminal *and* honest, had very good reasons for looking upon the Law with a dubious and distrustful eye.

Many of the cops Carella knew were non-discriminating. This did not mean they were unprejudiced. In fact, they were sometimes too *overly* democratic when it came to deciding exactly which citizen was in possession of a glassine bag of heroin lying on a sawdust-covered floor. If you were a black or a tan slum dweller, and a white cop entered the joint, the odds were six-to-five that he suspected all non-whites of using narcotics, and you could only pray to God that a nearby junkie (of *whatever* color) would not panic and dispose of his dope by dropping it at your feet. You also realized that, God forbid, you might just possibly bear a slight resemblance to a man who'd held up a liquor store or mugged an old lady in the park (white cops sometimes finding it difficult to distinguish one black man or one Puerto Rican from another) and end up at the old station house being advised of your rights and subjected to a strictly by-the-book interrogation that would crack Jesus Christ himself.

If you happened to be white, you were in even worse trouble. In the city for which Carella worked, most of the cops were white. They naturally resented all criminals (and slum dwellers were often automatically equated with criminals), but they especially resented *white* criminals, who were expected to know better than to run around making the life of a white cop difficult. The best thing a slum dweller could do when he smelled a cop approaching was get the hell out fast. Which is exactly what everybody in the bar did the moment Carella walked in. This did not surprise him; it had happened too often before. But it did leave him feeling somewhat weary, and resigned, and angry, and self-pitying, and sorrowful. In short, it left him feeling human – like the slum dwellers who had fled at his approach.

A white man and a black man were sitting together in a booth near the juke box. With the exception of the bartender and a hooker in hot pants (who wasn't worried about a bust, probably because her pimp had a fix in with the cop on the beat), they were the only two people who didn't immediately down their drinks and disappear. Carella figured them to be Lockhart and Barnes. He went over to the booth, introduced himself, and ordered a fresh round of drinks for them. Aside from their coloration, Lockhart and Barnes were similar in almost every other respect. Each man was in his early seventies, each was going bald, each had the veined nose and rheumy eyes of the habitual drinker, each had work-worn hands, each had a face furrowed with deep wrinkles and stamped indelibly with weariness and defeat, the permanent stigmata of a lifetime of grinding poverty and meaningless labor. Carella told them he was investigating the Grimm case and wanted to know everything they could remember about the night of the fire. Lockhart, the white man, looked at Barnes.

'Yes?' Carella said.

'Well, there's not much to tell,' Lockhart said.

'*Nothing* to tell, in fact,' Barnes said.

'As I understand it, you were both drugged.'

'That's right,' Lockhart said.

'That's right,' Barnes said.

'Want to tell me about that?'

'Well, there's not much to tell,' Lockhart said again.

'*Nothing* to tell, in fact,' Barnes said.

'We just passed out, that's all.'

'What time was that?'

'Little after ten, must've been. Isn't that right, Lenny?'

'That's right,' Barnes said.

'And you both got to work at eight, is that right?'

'Eight on the dot. Always try to relieve Frank right on time,' Lockhart said. 'It's a long enough day without having to wait for your relief.'

'Anybody come to the factory between eight and ten?'

'Not a soul,' Barnes said.

'None of those coffee-and-sandwich wagons, nothing like that?'

'Nothing,' Lockhart said. 'We make our own coffee. We got

a little hot plate in the room just off the entrance door there. Near where the wall phone is hanging.'

'And did you make coffee last Wednesday night?'

'We did.'

'Who made it?'

'Me,' Lockhart said.

'What time was that?'

'Well, we had a cup must've been about nine. Wasn't it about nine, Lenny?'

'Yeah, must've been about nine,' Barnes said, and nodded.

'Did you have another cup along about ten?'

'No, just that one cup,' Lockhart said.

'Just that one cup,' Barnes said.

'Then what?'

'Well, I went back outside again,' Lockhart said, 'and Lenny here went inside to make the rounds. Takes a good hour to go through the whole place, you know. There's four floors to the building.'

'So you had a cup of coffee at about nine, and then you went your separate ways, and you didn't see each other again until after the fire. Is that about it?'

'Well, we saw each other again,' Barnes said, and glanced at Lockhart.

'When was that?'

'When I finished my rounds, I came down and chatted awhile with Jim here.'

'What time was that?'

'Well, like Jim said, it takes about an hour to go through the building, so I guess it was about ten or a little before.'

'But you didn't have another cup of coffee at that time?'

'No, no,' Lockhart said.

'No,' Barnes said, and shook his head.

'What *did* you have?' Carella asked.

'Nothing,' Lockhart said.

'Nothing,' Barnes said.

'A shot of whiskey, maybe?'

'Oh, no,' Lockhart said.

'Ain't allowed to drink on the job,' Barnes said.

'But you *do* enjoy a little drink every now and then, don't you?'

'Oh, sure,' Lockhart said. '*Everybody* enjoys a little drink every now and then.'

'But not on the job.'

'No, never on the job.'

'Well, it's a mystery to me,' Carella said. 'Chloral hydrate works very fast, you see . . .'

'Yeah, it's a mystery to us, too,' Lockhart said.

'Yeah,' Barnes said.

'If you both passed out at ten o'clock . . .'

'Well, ten or a little after.'

'Are you *sure* you didn't have another cup of coffee? Try to remember.'

'Well, maybe we did,' Lockhart said.

'Yeah, maybe,' Barnes said.

'Be easy to forget a second cup of coffee,' Carella said.

'I think we must've had a second cup. What do you think, Lenny?'

'I think so. I think we must've.'

'But nobody came to the warehouse, you said.'

'That's right.'

'Then who put the knockout drops in your coffee?'

'Well, we don't know who could've done it,' Lockhart said.

'That's the mystery,' Barnes said.

'Unless you did it yourselves,' Carella said.

'What?' Lockhart said.

'Why would we do that?' Barnes said.

'Maybe somebody paid you to do it.'

'No, no,' Lockhart said.

'Nobody gave us a penny,' Barnes said.

'Then why'd you do it?'

'Well, we *didn't* do it,' Lockhart said.

'That's right,' Barnes said.

'Then who did it?' Carella asked. 'Who else *could* have done it? You were alone in the warehouse, it had to be one or both of you. I can't see any other explanation, can you?'

'Well, no, unless . . .'

'Yes?'

'Well, it might've been something else. Besides the coffee.'

'Like what?'

'I don't know,' Lockhart said, and shrugged.

'He means, like something else we didn't realize,' Barnes said.

'Something you drank, do you mean?'

'Well, maybe.'

'But you just told me you didn't drink anything but the coffee.'

'We're not allowed to drink on the job,' Barnes said.

'No one's suggesting you ever get *drunk* on the job,' Carella said.

'No, we never get drunk,' Lockhart said.

'But you do have a little nip every now and then, is that it?'

'Well, it gets chilly in the night sometimes.'

'Just to take the chill off,' Barnes said.

'You really didn't have a second cup of coffee, did you?'

'Well, no,' Lockhart said.

'No,' Barnes said.

'What *did* you have? A shot of whiskey?'

'Look, we don't want to get in trouble,' Lockhart said.

'*Did* you have a shot of whiskey? Yes or no?'

'Yes,' Lockhart said.

'Yes,' Barnes said.

'Where'd you get the whiskey?'

'We keep a bottle in the cabinet over the hot plate. In the little room near the wall phone.'

'Keep it in the same place all the time?'

'Yes.'

'Who else knows about that bottle?'

Lockhart looked at Barnes.

'Who else?' Carella said. 'Does Frank Reardon know where you keep that bottle?'

'Yes,' Lockhart said. 'Frank knows where we keep it.'

'Yes,' Barnes said.

*

There's nothing simpler to solve than an inside job, and this was shaping up as just that. Frank Reardon knew that the two nighttime shleppers hit the bottle, and he knew just where they stashed it. All he had to do was dose the booze, and then let nature take its course. Since one of the watchmen worked outside, any observer would know the minute the Mickey took effect.

Carella drove back over the Calm's Point Bridge, eager now to confront Reardon with the facts, accuse him of doctoring the sauce, and find out why he'd done it and whether or not he was working with anyone else. He parked the Chevy at the curb outside the warehouse and walked swiftly to the gate in the cyclone fence. The gate was unlocked, and so was the side entrance door to the building.

Frank Reardon lay just inside that door, two bullet holes in his face.

4

Carella eased the door shut behind him and drew his pistol. He did not know if Reardon's killer was still in the warehouse. He had been shot twice in his lifetime as a cop, both times unexpectedly, once by a punk pusher in Grover Park and again by a person known only as the Deaf Man. He had not particularly enjoyed either experience, since getting shot in reality is hardly ever like getting shot on television. He had no desire now to emulate Reardon's present condition; he stood stock-still, and listened.

A water tap was dripping someplace.

A fly buzzed around one of the sticky open holes in Reardon's face.

On the street outside, a truck ground into lower gear and labored up the hill from the river.

Carella listened and waited.

Three minutes passed. Five.

Cautiously, he stepped over Reardon's body, flattened himself against the wall, and edged his way past the telephone. The door to the adjacent small room was partially open. He could see a hot plate on a counter and above that a hanging wall cabinet. He shoved the door wide and allowed his gun hand to precede him into the room. It was empty. He came back up the corridor, stepped over Reardon's body again, and looked into the main storage area. Sodden ashes and charcoal, scorched metal tables, broken hanging light fixtures, nothing else. He kept the gun in his hand, went to the entrance door, and threw the slip bolt with his elbow. Ignoring Reardon for the moment, he went back to the small room in which Lockhart and Barnes had brewed their coffee and tippled their sauce. In the cabinet, he found a fifth of cheap whiskey. He put the gun down momentarily, wrapped part of his handkerchief around the neck of the bottle, a corner of it around the screw top, and twisted off the cap. Chloral hydrate has a slightly aromatic odor and a bitter taste, but all he could smell was alcohol fumes, and he wasn't about to take a swig of whatever was in that bottle. He screwed the cap back onto the bottle, put the handkerchief back into his pocket, and the .38 back into its holster. He tagged the bottle for later transmittal to the lab, and debated whether or not he should call Andy Parker and suggest that not only had he missed the probable cause of the fire, but he had also overlooked a bottle that most likely contained a sizable quantity of $CCl_3CHO.H_2O$. He went out into the hallway again.

Reardon was still lying on the floor, and Reardon was still dead.

The first bullet had taken him in the right cheek, the second one just below his nose, in the upper lip. The hole in the cheek was neat and small, the one below the nose somewhat messier because the bullet had torn away part of the lip, shattering teeth and gum ridge with the force of its entry. Carella didn't know any medical examiner who would risk his reputation by estimating the size of the bullet from the diameter of the hole left in the skin; bullets of different calibers often left entrance wounds of only slightly varying sizes. Nor did the size of the entrance wound always indicate from what distance the gun was fired; some small-caliber contact wounds, in fact, looked exactly like long-range shots. But there were powder grains embedded in Reardon's cheek and around his mouth, whereas there were no flame burns anywhere on his face. Carella guessed he'd been shot from fairly close up, but beyond the range of flame.

His initial supposition was that Reardon had opened the door on his killer and been surprised by a quick and deadly fusillade. But that didn't explain the unlocked gate in the cyclone fence. That gate had been padlocked when Carella visited the warehouse earlier today, and Reardon had opened it from the inside with a key from his belt ring. He had locked the gate again before leading Carella to the warehouse, and when the visit was over, he had walked back to the gate, unlocked it, let Carella out, and immediately locked it behind him again. So how had the killer got inside the fence? He would not have risked climbing it in broad daylight. The only answer was that Reardon had let him in. Which meant one of two things: either Reardon had known him and trusted him, or else the killer had presented himself as someone with good and valid reasons for being let inside.

Just inside the entrance door, Carella found two spent 9-mm cartridge cases, and left them right where they were for the moment. He went to the wall phone and dialed the precinct. He told Lieutenant Byrnes that he'd left Frank Reardon at approximately one-thirty that afternoon, and had returned to the warehouse not ten minutes ago to find him dead. The lieutenant advised Carella to stay there until the Homicide boys, the man from the ME's office, the lab technicians, and the police photographer arrived, which Carella would have done anyway. He asked if Hawes was back from Logan yet, and the lieutenant switched him over to the squadroom outside.

'Get anything up at Grimm's house?' Carella asked.

'Just one thing that may or may not be important,' Hawes said. 'There were no lights on until just before the fire.'

'That may tie in with what I found here.'

'You think it's the old electric-bulb gimmick?'

'Could be,' Carella said. 'I've also got a bottle that may or may not have chloral hydrate in it, a pair of spent 9-mm cartridge cases . . .'

'Oh-oh,' Hawes said.

'Right. We've got a homicide, Cotton.'

'Who?'

'Frank Reardon, day watchman here at the warehouse.'

'Any idea why?'

'Probably to shut him up. It's my guess he doctored the booze the night watchmen would be drinking. Do me a favor and run a routine check on him, will you?'

'Right. When're you coming back here?'

'The loot's contacting the clean-up boys now,' Carella said. 'Knowing them, I'll be here at least another hour. One more thing you can do while I'm gone.'

'What's that?'

'Run a check on Roger Grimm, too. If this was an inside job...'

'Got you.'

'I'll see you later. Few things I've got to tag and bag before the mob arrives.'

'Take your time. It's very quiet up here right now.'

*

It was not quiet when Carella got back to the squadroom at a quarter to six. Detectives Meyer and Brown had already come in to relieve the skeleton team, and they were busy in the corner of the room, yelling at a young man who sat with his right wrist handcuffed to a leg of the metal desk. Hawes was sitting at his own desk, oblivious of the noisy confrontation going on behind him. He looked up when Carella came through the gate.

'I've been waiting for you,' he said.

'So *do* you want a lawyer or *don't* you?' Brown shouted.

'I don't know,' the young man said. 'Tell me my rights again.'

'Jeee-sus *Christ*!' Brown exploded.

'Took a little longer than I expected,' Carella said.

'As usual,' Hawes said. 'Who'd Homicide send over? Monoghan and Monroe?'

'They're on vacation. These were two new guys, never saw them before. What'd you get from the IS?'

Meyer Meyer, hitching up his trousers, walked over to Hawes's desk. He was a burly man with china-blue eyes and a bald pate, which he mopped now with his handkerchief as he sat on the edge of the desk. 'Explained his rights four times,' he said. He held up his right hand like an Indian war bonnet. '*Four* goddamn times, can you imagine it? He *still* can't make up his mind.'

'Screw him,' Hawes said. '*Don't* tell him his rights.'

'Yeah, sure,' Meyer said.

'What'd he do?' Carella asked.

'Smash-and-grab. A jewelry store on Culver Avenue. Caught him with six wristwatches in his pocket.'

'So what's with the rights? You've got him cold. Book him and ship him out.'

'No, we want to ask him some questions,' Meyer said.

'What about?'

'He was carrying two decks of heroin. We'd like to know how he got them.'

'Same way as anybody else,' Hawes said. 'From his friendly neighborhood pusher.'

'Where've *you* been?' Meyer said.

'On vacation,' Hawes said.

'That explains it.'

'Explains what?'

'Why you don't know what's going on.'

'I hate mysteries,' Hawes said. 'You want to tell me what's going on, or you want to go back and explain that kid's rights to him?'

'Brown's doing that,' Meyer said, glancing over his shoulder. 'For the *fifth* time. I'd better go see if he's making any progress there,' he said, and walked back to where Brown was patiently explaining Miranda-Escobedo to the addict, who kept looking up at him solemnly.

'So what'd you get from the IS?' Carella asked Hawes.

'Nothing on Reardon, clean as a whistle.'

'What about Roger Grimm?'

'He took a fall six years ago.'

'What for?'

'Forgery/Three. He was working for an import-export house at the time, sold close to a hundred thousand dollars' worth of phony stock certificates before he got caught. Seventy-five thousand was recovered, stashed away in a bank.'

'What about the rest?'

'Spent it. Bought himself a new Cadillac, was living high on the hog at a hotel downtown on Jefferson.'

'Was he convicted?'

'Oh, sure. Sentenced to three years, and a two-thousand-dollar fine. Served a year and a half at Castleview, and was released on parole . . . Let me see,' Hawes said, and consulted his notes. 'Four years ago, this June.'

'How about since?'

'Nothing. Honest as the day is long.'

'Except that all of a sudden he has two fires.'

'Yeah, well, anybody can have a fire, Steve.'

'Anybody can sell phony stock certificates, too.'

'So where do we go from here?'

'I've got Reardon's address from his driver's license. I'd like to hit his apartment tomorrow morning, see what we can turn up there.'

'Okay. Shall we go together, or what?'

'What's tomorrow?'

'Friday. The sixteenth.'

'You take it alone, Cotton. I want to get a search warrant before the weekend, and the way the courts are jammed, I'm liable to be there all day.'

'What do you plan to do? Shake down Grimm's office?'

'Yeah, the Bailey Street place, where he keeps his books. That seems like the next logical step, don't you think?'

'Sounds good to me,' Hawes said.

'So let's go home.'

'Half-a-day today?' Meyer called from where he and Brown were still explaining Miranda-Escobedo to the kid.

'So what do you say, sonny?' Brown asked. 'You want to talk to us or not?' He was standing in his shirt sleeves near the chair in which the addict sat, his sleeves rolled up over power-ful forearms, a huge black man who dwarfed the kid sitting in the chair with his wrist handcuffed to the desk.

'What if I tell you about the scag?' the kid said. 'Will you forget about the wristwatches?'

'Now, sonny,' Brown said, 'you're asking us to make deals only the DA can make.'

'But you want to know about those two decks, don't you?'

'We're mildly interested,' Brown said, 'let me put it that way. We got you dead to rights on the burglary . . .'

'The robbery, you mean.'

'No, the burglary,' Brown said.

'I thought a burglary was when you went into somebody's apartment and ripped it off.'

'Sonny, I don't have time to give you a lecture on the Penal Law. You want the charge to read robbery, we'll be happy to oblige. You also got a rape or a homicide you want to tell us about, why, we'll just be tickled to death to listen. But Third-Degree Burglary is what we got you on, and that's what we're going to book you for. If that's okay with you.'

'Okay, fine,' the kid said.

'Now, if you want to cooperate with us,' Brown said, 'and I'm not making any promises because that's expressly forbidden by Miranda-Escobedo . . . but if you want to cooperate with us and talk about how you got that heroin, why maybe we can later whisper in the DA's ear that you were helpful, though I'm not making any promises.'

The kid looked up at Brown. He was a skinny kid with a longish nose and pale blue eyes and hollow cheeks. He was wearing dungarees and a striped, short-sleeved polo shirt. The hit marks of his addiction ran up the length of his arm, following the veins like an army of marauding ants.

'What do you say?' Brown asked. 'You're wasting our time here. If you want to talk to us, speak now or forever hold your peace. The sergeant downstairs is waiting to write your name in the book.'

'Well, I don't see no harm talking to you,' the kid said. 'Provided . . .'

'Never mind "provided",' Meyer said. 'He just told you we can't make any promises.'

'Well, I *realize* that,' the kid said, offended.

'Well, fine,' Meyer said. 'So shit or get off the pot, will you?'

'I *said* I'd talk to you.'

'Okay, so talk.'

'What do you want to know?' the kid asked.

'How about starting with your name?' Brown said.

'Samuel Rosenstein.'

'You Jewish?' Meyer said.

'Yes,' the kid said defensively. 'What of it?'

'You stupid son of a bitch,' Meyer said, 'why're you shooting that poison into your body?'

'What's it to you?' the kid said.

'Dumb bastard,' Meyer said, and walked away.

'All right, Sammy,' Brown said, 'how'd you get those two decks you were carrying?'

'If you think I'm going to tell you the name of my connection, we can quit talking right this minute.'

'I didn't ask you *who*, and I didn't ask you *where*. I asked you *how*.'

'I don't follow,' Sammy said.

'Now, Sammy,' Brown said, 'you and I both know that two weeks ago there was the biggest narcotics bust we've ever had in this city . . .'

'Oh, is that it?' Sammy said.

'Is *what* it?'

'Is that why it's so tough to score?'

'Don't you read the papers?' Brown asked.

'I ain't got time to read the papers. I just been noticing the stuff is scarce, that's all.'

'It's scarce because the 5th Squad busted a dope factory and confiscated two hundred kilograms waiting to be cut and packaged.'

'How much is that?'

'More than four hundred pounds.'

'Wow!' Sammy said. 'Four hundred pounds of scag? That could keep me straight for a year.'

'You and every other junkie in this city. You know how much that's worth pure?'

'How much?'

'Forty-four million dollars.'

'That's before they cut it, huh?'

'That's right. Before they put it on the street for suckers like you to buy.'

'I didn't ask to be a junkie,' Sammy said.

'No? Did somebody force it on you?'

'Society,' Sammy said.

'Bullshit,' Brown said. 'Tell me how you got those two decks.'

'I don't think I want to talk to you any more,' Sammy said.

'Okay, are we finished then? Meyer, the kid's ready for booking.'

'Okay,' Meyer said, and walked over.

'I been saving it,' Sammy said suddenly.

'How's that?'

'I been a junkie for almost three years now. I know there's good times and bad, and I always keep a little hid away. That was the last of it, those two decks. You think I'd've busted a store window if I wasn't desperate? Prices are skyrocketing, it's like a regular junk inflation. Listen, don't you think I *know* we're in for a couple of bad weeks here?'

'Couple of bad *months* is more like it,' Meyer said.

'Months?' Sammy said, and fell silent, and looked up at the two detectives. 'Months?' he said again, and blinked his eyes. 'That can't be. I mean . . . what's a person supposed to do if he can't . . . ? I mean, what's gonna happen to me?'

'You're going to break your habit, Sammy,' Brown said. 'In jail. Cold turkey.'

'What'll they give me for the burglary?' Sammy asked. His voice was quite low now; he seemed drained of all energy.

'Ten years,' Brown said.

'Is this a first offense?' Meyer asked.

'Yeah. I usually . . . I usually get money from my parents, you know? I mean, enough to get me through the week. I don't have to steal, they help me out, you know? But the prices are so high, and the junk is so lousy . . . I mean, you're paying twice as much for half the quality, it's terrible, I mean it. I know guys who're shooting all *kinds* of shit in their arms. It's a bad scene, I got to tell you.'

'How old are you, Sammy?' Meyer asked.

'Me? I'll be twenty on the sixth of September.'

Meyer shook his head and walked away. Brown unlocked the handcuff and led Sammy out of the squadroom, to where he would be booked for Third-Degree Burglary at the muster desk downstairs. He had told them nothing new.

'So now what?' Meyer said to Carella. 'Now we book him

on the smash-and-grab, and he'll be convicted, of course, and what did we accomplish? We sent another addict to prison. That's like sending diabetics to prison.' He shook his head again and, almost to himself, said, 'A nice Jewish boy.'

5

Frank Reardon had lived in an eight-story building on Avenue J, across the street from a huge multi-level parking lot. On Friday morning the electric company was tearing up the street outside in an attempt to get at some underground cables, and cars were stalled all up and down the avenue as Hawes rang the bell to the superintendent's apartment. The apartment was on street level, at the far end of a narrow alley on the left-hand side of the building. Even here, insulated from the street outside, Hawes could hear the insistent stutter of the pneumatic drills, the impatient honking of horns, the shouts of the motorists, the angry retorts of the men tearing up the street. He rang the bell again, unable to hear anything over the din and wondering if it was working.

The door opened suddenly. The woman standing there in the shaded doorway to the apartment was perhaps forty-five years old, a blond slattern wearing only a soiled pink slip and fluffy pink house slippers. She looked up at Hawes out of pale, cool green eyes, flicked an ash from her cigarette, and said, 'Yeah?'

'Detective Hawes,' he said, '87th Squad. I'm looking for the super.'

'I'm his wife,' the woman said. She dragged on her cigarette, let out a stream of smoke, studied Hawes again, and said, 'Mind showing me your badge?'

Hawes took out his wallet and opened it to where his shield was pinned to the leather opposite a lucite-encased identification card. 'Is your husband home?' he asked.

'He's downtown picking up some hardware,' the woman said. 'What can I do for you?'

'I'm investigating a homicide,' Hawes said. 'I'd like to take a look at Frank Reardon's apartment.'

'He kill somebody?' the woman asked.

'The other way around.'

'Figures,' she said knowingly. 'Let me put something on, and get the key.'

She went back into the apartment without closing the door. Hawes waited outside in the cool alleyway. The forecasters had predicted a high of ninety-four degrees, a humidity reading of eighty-one percent, and an unsatisfactory air-pollution level. On the street outside, the motorists were honking and yelling, and the drills were yammering. Through the open doorway, Hawes saw the woman pull the slip over her head. She had been naked under the garment, and she moved silently across the room now, her body flashing white as she receded deeper into the dimness. When she came back to the doorway, her hair was combed and she had put on fresh lipstick, a short green cotton smock, and white sandals.

'Ready?' she said.

He followed her out of the alley into the sudden blinding heat of the day, and then to the front door of the building and up the stairs to the third floor. The woman said nothing. The hallways and the steps were scrupulously clean and smelled of Lysol. At ten o'clock in the morning the building was silent. The woman stopped outside an apartment marked with the brass numerals *34*. As she unlocked the door, she said, 'How'd he get killed?'

'Someone shot him,' Hawes said.

'Figures,' the woman said, and opened the door, and led him into the apartment.

'He live here alone?' Hawes asked.

'All alone,' the woman said.

There were three rooms in the apartment: a kitchen, a living room, and a bedroom. Except for some dirty dishes in the sink and a bed that had been hastily made, the apartment was neat and clean. Hawes raised the shades on both living-room windows, and sunlight streamed into the room.

'What'd you say your name was?' the woman asked.

'Detective Hawes.'

'I'm Barbara Loomis,' she said.

The living room was sparsely and inexpensively furnished: a couch, an easy chair, a standing floor lamp, a television set.

An imitation oil painting of a shepherd and a dog in a pastoral landscape hung over the couch. An ashtray with several cigar butts in it was on the coffee table.

Barbara sat in one of the easy chairs and crossed her legs. 'Where'd you get that white streak in your hair?' she asked.

'I was stabbed by a building superintendent,' Hawes said.

'Really?' Barbara said, and laughed unexpectedly. 'You just can't trust supers,' she said, still laughing. 'Nor their wives, either,' she added, and looked at Hawes.

'Did Reardon smoke cigars?' he asked.

'I don't know what he smoked,' Barbara said. 'I still don't see why it's white.'

'They had to shave the hair to get at the wound. It grew back white.'

'It's cute,' Barbara said.

Hawes went out of the living room and into the bedroom. Barbara stayed in the easy chair, watching him through the doorframe. There was a bed, a dresser, an end table with a lamp on it, and a straight-backed chair over which was draped a striped sports shirt. A package of Camel cigarettes and a matchbook advertising an art school were in the pocket of the shirt. The bed was covered with a white chenille spread. Hawes pulled back the spread and looked at the pillows. There were lipstick stains on one of them. He went to what he assumed was the closet, and opened the door. Four suits, a sports jacket, and two pairs of slacks were hanging on the wooden bar. A pair of brown shoes and a pair of black shoes were on the floor. A blue woolen bathrobe was hanging on the door hook. On the shelf above the bar, there was a blue peaked cap and a gray fedora. Hawes closed the door and went to the dresser. Opening the top drawer, he asked, 'How long was Reardon living here?'

'Moved in about a year ago,' Barbara said.

'What kind of a tenant was he?'

'Quiet, for the most part. Brought women in every now and then, but who cared about that? Man's entitled to a little comfort every now and then, don't you think?'

The top drawer of the dresser contained handkerchiefs,

socks, ties, and a candy tin with a painted floral design. Hawes lifted off the cover. There were six sealed condoms in the tin, a photostated copy of Reardon's birth certificate, his discharge papers from the United States Navy, and a passbook for a savings account at one of the city's larger banks. Hawes opened the passbook.

'Can't say I cared much for the company he was keeping these past few weeks,' Barbara said.

'What kind of company was that?' Hawes asked.

'Coloreds,' Barbara said.

The passbook showed that Frank Reardon had deposited $5,000 in his account on August 2, five days before the warehouse fire. His previous deposits, on July 15 and June 24, had been for $42.00 and $17.00 respectively. The balance, before the $5,000 deposit, had been $376.44. Hawes put the passbook into his jacket pocket.

'I got nothing against coloreds,' Barbara said, 'so long as they stay uptown. He had these two big coloreds coming here, and last week he had this bitch come in stinking of perfume. Couldn't get her smell out of the hallway for a week. You should've seen her. Hair out to here, earrings down to here, skirt way up to here.' Barbara pulled her smock higher in illustration. 'Spent a couple of nights with him, used to wait for him outside the building till he got home from work.'

'When was this?' Hawes asked.

'Last week sometime.'

'Would you remember when last week?'

'Monday and Tuesday, I think. Yeah, both nights.'

'Do you know her name?'

'Frank didn't introduce me,' Barbara said. 'I'd have told her to get her black ass uptown, where she belongs.'

'And you say some black men were here, too?'

'Yeah. But not at the same time, you understand.'

'When were they here?'

'The last week in July sometime.'

'How many times were they here?'

'Two or three times.'

'How many men did you say?'

'Two of them. Black as the ace of spades. I ran into one of them once, he scared hell out of me.'

'How do you mean?'

'I mean the *look* of him. Big as a house, and wearing these clothes the coloreds think are so sharp, you know, and with a knife scar running clear down the left-hand side of his face. Drove up in a big white Caddy. I told my husband about him, and he said I'd better stay in the apartment whenever people like that were around. You know those coloreds, nothing they'd like better than to get their hands on a white woman. Especially a blonde,' Barbara said. 'Not that my husband's ever around to stop anybody from doing anything they *wanted* to do. He's always running downtown to Bridge Street, picking up hardware and electrical stuff on those sidewalk stalls they got down there. I could get raped here by half a *dozen* coloreds, he'd never know the difference.'

'Would you know the names of those two men?' Hawes asked.

'Nope. I'm not interested in knowing those kind of people, thank you. It's awfully hot in here, don't you think?'

'Supposed to hit ninety-four,' Hawes said, and opened the second dresser drawer.

'Thank God I've got air conditioning downstairs,' Barbara said. 'Only in the bedroom, but that's at least something.'

There were half a dozen shirts, a cardigan sweater, three pairs of undershorts, and two T-shirts in the second drawer. A white plastic battery-powered vibrator in the shape of a penis was tucked under the cardigan sweater. Hawes closed the drawer.

'What I'm going to do, soon as we finish here,' Barbara said, 'is go downstairs, pour myself a beer, and go hide in the bedroom, where the air conditioner is.'

Hawes opened the bottom drawer of the dresser. It was empty. He closed the drawer and walked to the night table on the left-hand side of the bed.

'I can't see you any more,' Barbara said from the living room, 'and I like to watch you work.' She suddenly appeared in the doorframe, arms folded across her midsection, cradling her breasts. 'That's better,' she said. She watched as Hawes opened the single drawer in the night table. There was a flashlight in the drawer, a half-empty carton of Camels, a box of wooden kitchen matches, and an address book.

'That husband of mine,' Barbara said, and hesitated.

Hawes opened the address book and quickly scanned it. Frank Reardon had not known too many people. There were perhaps a dozen listings in all, scattered alphabetically throughout the book. One of those was for a man who lived in Diamondback, uptown. His name was Charles Harrod, and his address was 1512 Kruger Street. The listing was significant only in that Diamondback was the city's largest black ghetto.

'Probably be gone all day,' Barbara said. 'My husband. Probably won't get home till suppertime.'

Hawes put the address book in his pocket with the passbook and walked back through the living room and into the kitchen. Stove, refrigerator, wooden table, cupboard over the sink. He glanced through the cupboard quickly.

'Hot as hell in here,' Barbara said. 'I'd open the windows, but I don't know if I'm allowed to. I mean, with Frank being dead and all.'

'I'm almost finished here,' Hawes said.

'I don't envy you men in the summertime,' Barbara said, 'having to wear suits and ties. I've got nothing at all on under this little thing, and I'm still suffocating.'

Hawes closed the cupboard doors, took a cursory look through the drawer in the kitchen table, and then turned to Barbara, who was standing near the refrigerator, watching him. 'Well, that's it,' he said. 'Thank you very much.'

'My pleasure,' she said, and walked silently out of the apartment. She waited for him to join her in the hallway, locked the door to Reardon's apartment, and then started down the steps ahead of Hawes. 'Nice cold bottle of beer'll really hit the spot now,' she said. She glanced over her shoulder, one hand on the banister, and said, almost shyly, 'You feel like joining me?'

'I've got to get uptown,' Hawes said. 'Thanks, anyway.'

'Nice and cool in my bedroom,' Barbara said. 'I got a nice air conditioner in there. Come on,' she said, and smiled. 'Give yourself a break. Little beer never hurt anybody.'

'Gee, I'd like to,' he said, 'but I've got a lot of work to do.'

'Well, okay,' she said, and went swiftly down the stairs. On the sidewalk outside, she said, 'Anything else you need, you know where to find me.'

'Thanks again,' Hawes said.

She seemed about to say something more. Instead, she nodded briefly, and went into the alley to her apartment, and her air-conditioned bedroom, and her bottle of beer.

*

The Police Department had advised all residents of the city that special spray attachments for fire hydrants were available at all precinct houses, and that any civic group could obtain them there free of charge, merely by applying. The idea behind this generous distribution of spray attachments was a good one. During the summertime people in the city's slums opened the hydrants full force in order to provide showers for their sweltering kids. This was good for the kids but bad for the firemen. The open hydrants, you see, drastically reduced the water pressure needed for fire-fighting. Since the spray attachments needed very little water in order to operate effectively, they seemed like a logical and fair compromise.

But what excitement was there in *legally* obtaining one of those attachments from the fuzz, when it was just as simple to screw off the nozzle caps with a monkey wrench, open the octagonal brass valve on top of the hydrant, and then tilt the end of a wooden orange crate against the high-pressure stream of water that roared from the open spout, providing a city waterfall of spectacular proportions? If, as a result, a tenement down the street happened to burn down because the firemen didn't have enough water pressure when they attached their hoses – well, that was one of the prices a slum dweller had to pay for his summertime fun and games. Besides, most slum fires occurred in the dead of winter, caused by cheap, faulty heaters and bad electrical wiring.

The hydrants all up and down Kruger Street were on as

Hawes made his way up the block. Black boys and girls in bathing suits splashed in and out of the icy cold cascades, while grownups sat on front stoops and fire escapes, fanning themselves and watching in envy. It was only a quarter to eleven in the morning, but the temperature had already soared to ninety-one degrees, and the air was stifling. 1512 Kruger was a red-brick tenement with a Baptist storefront church on one side of it and a billiard parlor on the other. Three young men wearing blue denim gang jackets were standing outside the green-painted, plate-glass window of the pool hall, watching the younger kids frolicking in the water at the nearest open johnny pump. They glanced at Hawes as he climbed the three steps to the front stoop of the building. A fat black man in a white undershirt sat against the iron railing, fanning himself with a copy of *Ebony*, holding a bottle of Coca-Cola in which there were two twisted straws. The street gang members knew that Hawes was a cop. So did the fat man in the white undershirt. This was a slum.

Hawes went into the vestibule and checked the mailboxes. There were twelve boxes in the row. Eight had broken locks. Only one of them had a name in the space provided, and the name was *not* Charles Harrod's. Hawes came out onto the stoop again. The street gang members had disappeared. The fat man was watching the kids playing under the water.

'Good morning,' Hawes said.

'Morning,' the man replied briefly. He put both straws between his lips, sipped from the bottle, and kept looking at the kids.

'I'm looking for a man named Charles Harrod . . .'

'Don't know him,' the man said.

'He's supposed to live in this building . . .'

'Don't know him,' the man repeated. He had not taken his eyes from the children playing near the fire hydrant.

'I was wondering if you knew what apartment he lived in.'

The man turned and looked up at Hawes. 'I just told you I don't know him,' he said.

'Know where I can find the super of the building?'

'Nope,' the fat man said.

'Thanks a lot,' Hawes said, and walked down the flat steps to the pavement. He wiped the back of his hand across his sweating upper lip, and then went into the pool hall. There were two tables in the place, one of them empty, one of them occupied by the gang members he had seen standing outside a few minutes ago. Hawes walked over to the table. 'I'm looking for a man named Charles Harrod,' he said. 'Any of you fellows know him?'

A young man, leaning over the table, stick in hand, said, 'Never heard of him,' and triggered off a shot that sank two balls and left the cue ball in position for an easy chip shot. He was tall and thin, sporting a black beard and mustache, the back of his denim jacket ornately painted with the name of the gang – *The Ancient Skulls* – curving over an appropriate painting of a grinning white skull and crossbones. Hawes thought he had seen the last of the street gangs twenty years ago, but he supposed all good things – like plagues and locusts – returned at regularly spaced intervals.

'He's supposed to live in the building next door,' Hawes said.

'We don't live in the building next door,' another of the young men said. He was bigger than the bearded one, almost as big as Hawes, the pool cue looking undersized in his enormous hands.

'Where *do* you live?' Hawes asked.

'Who wants to know?'

'I'm a police officer, let's cut the crap,' Hawes said.

'We're shooting a friendly game of pool here,' the bearded one said, 'and we don't know Charlie whatever-his-name-is . . .'

'Harrod.'

'We don't know him. So, like, what's the beef, Officer?'

'None at all,' Hawes said. 'What's your name?'

'Avery Evans.'

'And you?' Hawes said, turning to the big one.

'Jamie Holder.'

'And none of you know Harrod, huh?'

'None of us,' Holder said.

'Okay,' Hawes said, and walked out.

The fat man was still sitting on the stoop. His Coke bottle was empty and he had placed it between his shoes. Hawes climbed onto the stoop and went into the vestibule. He opened the broken glass door dividing the vestibule from the inner hallway, and then started up the flight of steps to the first floor. The hallway stank of urine and cooking smells. He rapped at the first door he came to, and a woman inside said, 'Who is it?'

'Police officer,' he said. 'Want to open up, please?'

The door opened a crack. A woman with her hair tied in rags peered into the hallway. 'What is it?' she said. 'Nothing's happened to Fred, has it?'

'Nothing's happened to anybody,' Hawes said. 'I'm looking for a man named Charles Harrod . . .'

'I don't know him,' the woman said, and closed the door.

Hawes stood in the hallway a moment longer, debating whether he should go through this routine with every apartment in the building, and finally decided to go find a cop. He found one up the block, near the corner, a black patrolman turning off the fire hydrant there with a monkey wrench. Kids in swimming trunks danced around him as the patrolman worked, sweating in his blue uniform, armpits stained. They shouted at him, and taunted him, and splashed their feet in the curbside puddles, hoping to get him as wet as they were, but he steadfastly turned the octagonal brass fitting until the stream of water became a trickle and then stopped entirely. He screwed both heavy iron caps back onto the hydrant, and then fitted a new lock into place, a lock that would be broken before the day was out, just as its predecessor had been broken.

'You want to use the hydrants, go get a spray attachment,' he said to the assembled kids.

'Go hump your mother,' one of the kids said.

'I *already* humped yours,' the patrolman answered, and began walking up the block toward the next hydrant.

Hawes fell into step beside him. 'Got a minute?' he said, and flashed his detective's shield.

'What's up?' the patrolman asked.

'I'm looking for a man named Charles Harrod, 1512 Kruger. Would you know what apartment he's in?'

'Harrod, Harrod,' the patrolman said. 'Big guy, white Cadillac, tailor-made suits, knife scar down the left side of his face. That the one?'

'Sounds like him.'

'Building near the pool parlor,' the patrolman said. 'Is that 1512?'

'That's 1512.'

'He lives on the top floor, I don't know the apartment number. There's only two apartments on each floor, so you can't go wrong.'

'Thanks, pal,' Hawes said.

'Don't mention it,' the patrolman said, and walked off carrying his monkey wrench. Up the block, the kids had already seen him coming and were already starting to chant.

Hawes went back to the building. Inside the church next door, the congregation had begun singing. The fat man on the stoop was tapping his foot in time to the music. He knocked over the Coke bottle and bent to pick it up as Hawes went past him again and into the dark vestibule. The heat on the upper stories of the building was stifling. Hawes reached the sixth floor and knocked on the door nearest to the stairwell. There was no answer. He knocked again, and this time a voice said, 'Who's there?' The voice was pitched very low; he could not tell if it belonged to a man or a woman.

'Charlie?' he said.

'Charlie ain't here right now,' the voice said. 'Who's that, anyway?'

'Police officer,' Hawes said. 'Mind opening the door?'

'Go away,' the voice said.

'I've got a warrant for the arrest of Charles Harrod,' Hawes lied. 'Open the door, or I'll kick it in.'

'Just a minute,' the voice said.

Hawes moved against the wall to the side of the door – just in case the voice inside *was* Charlie Harrod's, and just in case Harrod had shot Frank Reardon to death, and just in case his lie about the warrant resulted in a fusillade of bullets through the wooden door. He unbuttoned his jacket and cleared his holster. Footsteps were approaching the door. The door opened wide.

A young black girl was standing in the doorway, back-lighted with strong sunlight that blazed through an open kitchen window. She was wearing dungarees and a pink halter top. She was tall and slender, with long narrow fingers and an Afro hairdo that billowed from her head like a cloud of smoke. Her eyes were brown and savvy and distrustful and angry. In her low, hoarse voice, she immediately asked, 'Where's the warrant?'

'I haven't got one,' Hawes said. 'Does Charles Harrod...?'

'Goodbye,' the girl said, and started to close the door.

Hawes stuck his foot into it. 'Don't make me go all the way downtown for one, honey,' he said. 'I get mean as hell when I have to go to all that trouble.'

The girl, holding the door against his foot with all her strength, said, 'I told you Charlie ain't here. I don't know where he's at.'

'Let's talk about it,' Hawes said.

'Nothing to talk about.'

'Back away from that door before I knock you on your ass,' Hawes said.

'I know my rights.'

'You can tell me all about them at the station house, when I claim you tried to slash my face with a razor blade.'

'What razor blade? Man, that's pure shit, and you know it.'

'The razor blade I keep right here in my jacket pocket, just for situations like this one. You want to open that door, or do I kick it in and bring assault charges?'

'Man, you're really something,' the girl said, and opened the door wide. 'Okay,' she said, 'let's see it.'

'The razor blade?'

'The badge, man, the badge.'

Hawes opened his wallet. She studied his shield and his ID card, and then turned her back, walked into the apartment, and went directly to the sink, where she opened the faucet and let the water run. Hawes followed her inside closing and locking the door behind him. The kitchen was small and badly in need of a paint job, but bright with sunshine that streamed through the open window. A cheesebox with geraniums in it sat on the fire escape outside. The refrigerator had been painted a pastel blue, and was in one corner of the room alongside an ancient gas stove. The sink and hanging cabinets were on the wall obliquely opposite the window. A wooden table and two chairs were against the other wall. A telephone rested on top of an Isola directory on the table.

'Does Charlie Harrod live here?' he asked.

'He lives here.'

'Who're you?'

'A friend.'

'What kind of friend?'

'A *girl* kind of friend.'

'What's your name?'

'Elizabeth.'

'Elizabeth what?'

'Benjamin. You really got a blade in your coat?'

'Sure.'

'Let me see it.'

Hawes reached into his jacket pocket and removed from it a single-edged razor blade with a thin protective cardboard shield over the cutting edge. He did not tell Elizabeth that the blade was a working tool rather than a weapon; in the course of an investigation, he frequently had to open cartons or cut twine or slit the clothing of a bleeding victim.

'You're really something else,' Elizabeth said, and shook her head.

'Is that water running for a reason?' Hawes asked.

'Yeah, I'm thirsty, that's the reason,' Elizabeth said. She took a glass from the drain board on the sink, filled it to the brim, and began drinking. But she did not turn off the faucet.

'Why don't we go in the other room?' Hawes said.

'What for?'

'More comfortable in there.'

'I'm comfortable right here. You don't like the accommodations, you're free to leave.'

'Let's talk about Charlie Harrod.'

'I told you before, there's nothing to talk about.'

'Where does he work?'

'Haven't the faintest.'

'*Does* he work?'

'I suppose so. You'll have to ask him yourself.'

'Where can I find him?'

'Haven't the faintest.'

'You mind if I turn off that water? I'm having trouble hearing you.'

'If I don't let it run, it won't be cold,' Elizabeth said. 'Anyway, it's quiet water, we can hear each other fine.'

'Who *else* can hear us, Elizabeth?'

The question startled her. He had suspected the apartment was bugged from the moment she refused to turn off the tap or go into the other room. She had not moved from her position near the sink, which could mean that the bug was somewhere in the wall cabinet, probably under the wooden trim, and the sound of running water would overwhelm the sensitive mike and obliterate any other sound in the room. But if the apartment was bugged, who was bugging it? And if she knew the location of the bug, why hadn't she simply ripped it out?

'Ain't nobody here but the two of us,' she said, regaining her composure. 'Who else *could* hear us?'

'Walls have ears these days,' Hawes said, and walked to the sink, and turned off the tap.

Elizabeth immediately moved to the other side of the room, away from the sink and facing the open window. When she spoke, her voice was directed toward the fire escape. 'I've got things to do,' she said. 'If you're finished here, I'd like to get dressed.'

'Mind if I look around a little?'

'For that, you *do* need a warrant, mister.'

'I can get one, you know.'

'For what? Charlie do something against the law?'

'Maybe.'

'Then go get your warrant, man. I sure wouldn't want no criminal to be escaping justice.'

'Know a man named Frank Reardon?' Hawes asked, and again the question startled Elizabeth. Facing the open window, her back to him, her arms folded, he saw the slight involuntary hunching of her shoulders, as though someone had suddenly put an ice cube to the base of her neck.

'Frank *who*?' she said to the fire escape.

'Reardon.'

'Don't know him,' Elizabeth said.

'Ever wear earrings?' he asked her.

'Sure.'

'Perfume?'

'Sure.'

'Ever go downtown, Elizabeth? Like in the neighborhood of Avenue J and Allen?'

'Never.'

'Across the street from the big garage?'

'Never.'

'Happen to be there last Monday and Tuesday night?'

'*Never* been there.'

'What do you do for a living?' Hawes asked.

'I'm unemployed.'

'How old are you?'

'Twenty-four.'

'Ever work?'

'I used to be a waitress.'

'When was that?'

'Few years ago.'

'Haven't worked since?'

'Nope.'

'How do you support yourself?'

'I got friends,' Elizabeth said.

'Like Charlie Harrod?'

'Charlie's a friend, yes.'

'Frank Reardon's dead,' Hawes said, and watched the back of her neck.

This time she was ready. Without missing a beat, she said, 'I don't know any Frank Reardon, but of course I'm sorry to hear he's dead.'

'Tell Charlie when you see him, will you? He might be interested.'

'I'll tell him, but I doubt he'll be interested.'

Hawes turned toward the cabinet hanging over the sink. 'This is Detective Cotton Hawes, 87th Squad,' he said, 'investigating arson and homicide, concluding the questioning of Elizabeth Benjamin at exactly' – he looked at his watch – 'eleven twenty-three AM on Friday, August sixteen.' He turned to Elizabeth. 'Make it easier for them,' he said.

'I don't know what you're talking about,' Elizabeth said.

'Tell Charlie I'm looking for him,' Hawes said.

He unlocked the door, went out into the hallway, and closed the door behind him. Immediately he put his ear to the wood and listened. He heard nothing at first, and then he heard the water tap running, and then nothing again. He did not hear Elizabeth dialing the telephone, but that's exactly what she must have done, because the next thing he heard was her voice saying, 'Charlie, this is Liz. We just had a visit from the fuzz.' Silence. In that moment of silence, Hawes tried to understand what was happening. If they knew about the bug over the sink, they undoubtedly knew the phone would be tapped as well. Yet Elizabeth felt free enough on the instrument to tell Charlie they had just had a visit from the police. Had they unscrewed the mouthpiece and removed the mike? 'When will you be leaving there?' Elizabeth asked, and then said, 'Wait for me downstairs. I'll be over in ten minutes.' Hawes heard her replacing the receiver on its cradle. He moved away from the door and went swiftly down the steps to the street.

*

She had changed into her street clothes, a short blue skirt, a red-ribbed jersey top without a bra, high-heeled navy-blue patent-leather pumps, dangling earrings, and a red-leather sling bag. She stepped high and fast, and he had trouble keeping up with her. If she wasn't a hooker, he would eat his shield and his service revolver.

The streets of Diamondback were teeming with a populace driven outdoors by the heat; however hot it was on the sidewalk, it was hotter inside the tenements. There is no relief in the slums. In the summer you are hot, and in the winter you are cold. Summer or winter, spring or fall, you are infested with roaches and plagued with rats, and you are reminded constantly that you are an animal because you are forced to *live* like one. If Clearview across the river had been euphemistically named, Diamondback was a true and apt label for an area as deadly as a coiled rattlesnake.

Hawes walked on the opposite side of the street, following Elizabeth at a discreet distance, never losing sight of her. He walked past pimps in fancy dude threads, and he walked past men who were cabdrivers and letter carriers and sanitation employees; he walked past junkies sitting on the front stoops of boarded tenements and staring vacantly into space, nodding with their dreams of an America realized only in dope fantasies; he walked past candy stores taking numbers bets, and past women rushing home with grocery bags before heading downtown to work cleaning white apartments; he walked past young girls peddling their asses; he walked past young men in gang jackets and old men sitting on wooden crates, watching their shoes, and young men shooting dice on a hallway blanket, and men who were bootblacks and lavatory attendants and some who worked for ad agencies downtown (but who had trouble getting a taxi uptown after work, unless a brother was a hackie); he walked past short-order cooks and pushers, waiters and train conductors and muggers. He walked past honest men and thieves, victims and victimizers alike, who in their desperation called each other 'brothers' though the only thing that linked them together was the color of their skins.

Hawes did not share the opinion of those who believed that slums were exciting because at least they were alive. The way Hawes looked at it, slums were at least *dying*, if not already *dead*. The idea depressed and angered him as much as any assault or homicide would. He wondered why it did not depress or anger those men in high government positions who, instead,

68

seemed to prefer looking away from what was an open, bleeding, possibly fatal wound.

Go make your speeches on your high podiums, Hawes thought, in your blue serge suit and your polished brown shoes. Promise us equality and justice and tell us how the poorest son of a bitch on our welfare rolls would be considered a wealthy man in a nation someplace that's just coming out of the Stone Age. Grin, and shake all the hands, and exhibit your smiling wife, and tell us what a tireless campaigner she was, and explain how we are a nation on the edge of greatness. Tell us everything's all right, pal. Assure us, and reassure us. And then take a walk here in Diamondback. And keep your eyes on that girl ahead, because she is most likely a hooker, and she is living with a man who may be involved in a homicide, and *that* is America, too, and it isn't going to change simply because you tell us everything's all right, pal, when we know everything may just possibly be all wrong.

The girl stopped on the corner to talk to two men, jostling one of them with her hip, giggling, and then moving on again with her practiced prance, tight little behind wiggling in the short skirt, high-heeled pumps tapping a rapid tattoo on the pavement. On the corner of Mead and Landis, she went into a three-story tenement that had been converted into an office building. Hawes took up position in a doorway across the street. There were three street-side windows on each floor of the building Elizabeth had entered. On the first floor of the building, the middle window was lettered in gold with the words ARTHUR KENDALL, ATTORNEY AT LAW, the flanking windows decorated with large red seals and the words NOTARY PUBLIC. Two of the windows on the second floor of the building had been painted out; the middle window read DIAMONDBACK DEVELOPMENT, INC. The third floor of the building was occupied by a firm that announced itself, in fancy script lettering, as BLACK FASHIONS.

Elizabeth came out of the building not a moment after she had entered it.

She came out at a dead run, shoulder bag flying, skirt riding high on her long legs as she ran in seeming panic up the street. Hawes did not try to stop her. He crossed the street quickly and went into the building. A well-dressed black man was lying in the lobby, bleeding onto the broken blue-and-white-tile flooring. His eyes were rolled up in his head and he was staring sightlessly at the naked light bulb in the ceiling. A four-inch-long scar ran jaggedly through the cuts and bruises and open bleeding wounds on his face.

Hawes figured he had found Charlie Harrod.

6

In Roger Grimm's office, downtown on Bailey Street, Carella did not yet know that another body had turned up in Diamondback. All he knew was that two arsons and a homicide had already been committed, and that Roger Grimm had a police record. (It was true, of course, that Grimm had paid his debt to society. But some debts can never be paid, and a police record is rather like a stray wolf you've taken in on a dark and snowy night: it follows you for the rest of your life.)

Carella had spent all morning in court and was armed with a search warrant, but he preferred not to use it unless he had to. His reasoning was simple. Grimm was a suspect, but he did not want Grimm to know that. And so both men went through a pointless dialogue: Carella trying to hide the fact that he already had a warrant in the pocket of his jacket lest Grimm suspect he was a suspect; and Grimm trying to hide scrutiny of his records, a maneuver suspicious in itself.

'When did I become a suspect in this?' he asked, straight for the jugular.

'No one's even suggesting that,' Carella said.

'Then why do you want to go through my files?'

'You're anxious to clear up this business with the insurance company, aren't you?' Carella said. 'I assume you've got nothing to hide ...'

'That's right.'

'Then what's the problem?'

'I'm a businessman,' Grimm said. 'I've got competitors. I don't know whether I like the idea of someone having access to my files.'

'Consider me a priest,' Carella said, and smiled.

Grimm did not smile back.

'Or a psychiatrist,' Carella said.

'I'm not religious, and I'm not crazy,' Grimm said.

'I'm merely trying to say ...'

'I know what you're trying to say.'

'That I'm not about to run to the nearest importer of little wooden animals and reveal the inner workings of your operation. I'm investigating arson and homicide. All I want . . .'

'What've my records got to do with arson and homicide?'

'Nothing, I hope,' Carella said. 'Frankly, I'd like nothing better than to go through them and be able to report to your insurance company . . .'

'Companies.'

'*Companies*, that you're clean. Isn't that what *you* want, too, Mr Grimm?'

'Yes, but . . .'

'Officially, the warehouse arson is Parker's case. Officially, the fire in Logan belongs to the Logan police. But the Reardon homicide is mine. Okay, I'm here for two reasons, Mr Grimm. First, I'd like to help you with your insurance company . . . *companies*. That's why you came to me, Mr Grimm, remember? To get help, remember?'

'I remember.'

'Okay. So if, first, I can help establish your innocence with the insurance people, and, second, get a lead onto the homicide, I'll go home happy. What do you say, Mr Grimm? You want to send me home happy, or you want my wife and kids to eat with a grouch tonight?'

'My books and my correspondence are my business,' Grimm said, 'not the Police Department's.'

'When Parker gets back from vacation, he'll probably want to look at them, anyway. And he can get a warrant, if he has to.'

'Then tell him to get one. Or go get one yourself.'

'I've already got one,' Carella said, and handed it to him.

Grimm read it in silence. He looked up and said, 'So what was the song and dance?'

'We try to be friendly, Mr Grimm,' Carella said. 'You want to unlock your file cabinets, please?'

If Grimm had anything to hide, it was not immediately apparent to Carella. According to his records, he had started the import business in January, eight months ago, with a capital investment of $150,000 ...

'Mr Grimm,' Carella said, looking up from the ledger, 'the last time we talked, you told me you'd come into some money last year. Would that be the hundred and fifty thousand you used to start this business?'

'That's right,' Grimm said.

'How'd you happen to come into it?'

'My uncle died and left it to me. You can check if you like. His name was Ralph Grimm, and the will was settled last year, in September.'

'I'll take your word for it,' Carella said, and went back to the ledger. He had no intention of taking Grimm's word for anything.

The first business transaction listed in Grimm's books was for the initial purchase of a hundred thousand little wooden beasties back in January. There was a sheaf of related correspondence starting in December, in which Grimm haggled back and forth over the price with a man named Otto Gülzow of Gülzow Aussenhandel Gesellschaft in Hamburg. There was also a customs receipt indicating that Grimm had paid an eight-percent duty at the port of entry. There were three separate canceled checks: one for 37,120 marks paid to the order of Gülzow Aussenhandel and totaling approximately ten percent of the agreed-upon purchase price (presumably to cover Gülzow for the risk of packing and shipping); another for 9,280 American dollars paid to the order of the Bureau of Customs; and the last, a certified check for 334,080 marks, paid to the order of Gülzow, and dated January 18, presumably the date the shipment had been handed over to Grimm. The three checks totaled close to $125,000, the price Grimm had said he'd paid for the first shipment. Everything seemed in order. An honest businessman doing business, legally shipping in his little wooden creatures, paying the import duty, and then selling them to retail outlets all over the United States.

According to Grimm's records, the wooden menagerie had indeed caught on like crazy. His files substantiated that there had been orders for the entire first shipment, and payments to his firm (which incidentally was called Grimports, Inc., Carella realized with a wince) totaling $248,873.94, somewhat less than the $250,000 Grimm had estimated but close enough to establish his veracity. There followed another batch of correspondence with Herr Gülzow, during which Grimm argued for a lower price on the next shipment, since he was ordering twice as many little wooden dogs, cats, turtles, rabbits, horses, etc. Gülzow argued back in Teutonically stiff English that no discount was possible, since he himself purchased the carvings at exorbitant prices from peasants who whittled them in cottages here and there throughout the Fatherland. They finally compromised on a price somewhat higher than what Grimm had desired. Again, there was a canceled check for ten percent of the purchase price, a check to the Bureau of Customs, and a certified check to Gülzow Aussenhandel. Again the total came near to the $250,000 Grimm had stated to be the cost of the second shipment from Germany. This had been the shipment lost in the warehouse fire.

In corroboration of Grimm's earlier statement, there were orders from retail stores all over the country for the entire stock on hand, and there was return correspondence from Grimm promising delivery on or about August 12. There was also a new batch of correspondence with Gülzow, ordering another 400,000 of the animals, at a further slightly reduced price, and several letters from Grimm instructing that the shipment should be delivered first to a packing firm in Bremerhaven, since a portion of the previous shipment had arrived partially damaged and he wished to make certain this did not happen again. Grimm was quick to assure Gülzow that he was in no way holding Gülzow Aussenhandel responsible for the damage en route, but that since precautionary packing measures would be costing him 6,000 marks, could not Gülzow adjust the price on the new shipment to take into account this additional expense? Gülzow promptly replied that his firm 'packed quite well the animals', and that any additional packing Grimm felt necessary would have to be undertaken at his own expense. It was agreed that the animals would be sent to Bachmann Speditionsfirma, a packing house in Bremerhaven, on or about July 15, and that Bachmann would in turn ship them to the United States. Gülzow asked for the customary ten-percent check before sending the goods to Bachmann. There was a canceled check in the files, indicating that Grimm had complied with the request on July 9.

There was also a sheaf of correspondence with Erhard Bachmann, the Bremerhaven packer, chronologically overlapping the letters to and from Gülzow. The first letter in the Bachmann file outlined the method of packing he proposed to use; the carvings would first be individually wrapped in straw-filled brown paper, and then packed in wooden crates stuffed with excelsior. A condition of the contract with Bachmann (dated July 3) was that he would be held financially responsible for any portion of the shipment that arrived in anything less than perfect condition. Grimm's letter in reply agreed to the method of packing. The next letter from Bachmann advised Grimm that he had received the 400,000 animals from Hamburg on July 17, and was proceeding to pack them as per instructions. The last letter was dated July 26, and advised Grimm that the animals had been packed and would be shipped aboard the cargo vessel *Lottchen* leaving Bremerhaven on August 21 and arriving in America on August 28. It further mentioned that Bachmann had been advised through Gülzow that a certified check in the amount of 1,336,320 marks was expected to be turned over to his company representative at the port of entry before delivery of the cargo was made. There was only one puzzling paragraph in Bachmann's letter. The paragraph said:

We have today received your payment for packing as per our contract of July 3, for which thank you. Please be assured the cargo will reach you in excellent order.

Carella searched through the canceled checks again. He could find no check made out to Bachmann Speditionsfirma. He glanced up at Grimm, who was sitting at his desk and watching Carella in silence.

'This payment Bachmann mentions,' Carella said. 'When was it made?'

'Sometime at the end of last month,' Grimm said.

'I don't see a canceled check for it.'

'It sometimes takes time for checks to clear,' Grimm said. 'Payment was made in marks. Where foreign exchange is involved . . .'

'Well, this is the sixteenth of August,' Carella said. 'It should have cleared by now, don't you think?'

'It should have, but it hasn't. I'm not in charge of international banking,' Grimm said with some irritation.

'Mind if I see the stub for the check you wrote?' Carella asked.

'The checkbook is in the top drawer of the filing cabinet on your left,' Grimm said.

Carella opened the file drawer and took out the company checkbook. 'July when, did you say?'

'I'm not sure of the exact date.'

Carella had already opened the checkbook and was leafing through the stubs. 'Is this it,' he asked. 'Six thousand marks made payable to Bachmann Speditionsfirma on July 24?'

'Yes, that's the check.'

'He sure got it fast enough,' Carella said.

'What do you mean?' Grimm said.

'You sent the check on July 24. He acknowledges receipt of it in his letter of July 26.'

'That's not unusual,' Grimm said. 'The mails between here and Europe are very fast.'

'Are you saying it normally takes only two days for a letter to get from here to Germany?'

'Two days, three days,' Grimm said, and shrugged.

'I thought it was more like five days, six days.'

'Well, I don't keep track of how long it takes a letter to get there. Sometimes it's faster, sometimes it's slower.'

'This time it was faster,' Carella said.

'That's what it looks like. Unless Bachmann made a mistake in dating his letter. That's possible, too. These Germans pride themselves on their efficiency, but sometimes they make incredibly stupid mistakes.'

'Like mistakenly dating a letter acknowledging a check, right?'

'You'd be surprised at the mistakes they make,' Grimm said.

Carella said nothing. He turned back to the ledger and the file of correspondence. The next sheaf consisted of carbons of Grimm's letters to the Allied Insurance Company of America and originals of their letters to him. He had apparently begun doing business with them in June, when he had requested a schedule of rates for insuring 200,000 carved wooden animals, worth half a million dollars, while they were awaiting shipment from his warehouse. Allied had written back to ask for verification of the value of the stock, which he had supplied by sending them Xerox copies of the orders he had on hand. They had then informed him that $500,000 was a rather large risk for one company to take, and that they would be willing to share the risk with Mutual Assurance of Connecticut if Grimm was amenable to this arrangement. There then followed several letters in a similar vein between Grimm and Mutual Assurance, and the whole thing was finally settled by the end of June, with Grimm getting his insurance shortly before the second shipment arrived from Germany. There was no record in the files of Grimm having insured the *first* shipment. It almost seemed he was *expecting* a fire the second time around.

'I notice you didn't insure that first shipment,' Carella said. 'The one in January.'

'Couldn't afford it,' Grimm said. 'I had to take my chances.'

'Lucky you insured the second batch,' Carella said dryly.

'Yeah,' Grimm said. 'If they *pay* me. If they don't, I'm not so sure how lucky I was.'

'Oh, they'll pay you sooner or later,' Carella said. He closed the ledger and began copying the addresses, telephone numbers, cable addresses, and Telex numbers of both German firms into his notebook.

'Later isn't soon enough,' Grimm said.

'Well,' Carella said, and shrugged.

'What'll it take?' Grimm asked suddenly.

'What'll *what* take?'

'To get a clean bill of health from you.'

'I'm not sure my word alone would convince your insurers that . . .'

'But it would help, wouldn't it ?'

'Maybe, maybe not. What would *really* help is if we caught the arsonist. *And* the man who killed Frank Reardon. Assuming they're one and the same, which they might not be.'

'I think if you went to them and told them I had nothing to do with the fire, they'd release the money,' Grimm said. He was standing just directly to the left of where Carella sat now, looking down at him intently. 'Will you do it ?'

'No,' Carella said. 'I don't know *who* burned down your warehouse, Mr Grimm. Not yet, I don't.'

'How much ?' Grimm said.

'What ?'

'I said how *much*.'

The office went still.

'I'll pretend I didn't hear that,' Carella said.

'I meant how much *time*,' Grimm said quickly. 'How much *time* will you need to . . . ?'

'I'm sure you did,' Carella said. He rose, put on his jacket, and went to the door. 'If that canceled check shows up, give me a ring,' he said, and left the office. He had not mentioned Grimm's police record, and Grimm had not volunteered the information. But then again, if everybody was always totally honest with everybody else, Diogenes wouldn't have had a job, either.

*

Meanwhile, back at the scene of the crime, Hawes was going through the building at 2914 Landis Avenue with a detective from the 83rd Squad, in which precinct Diamondback happened to be located. The detective was named Oliver Weeks. He was affectionately called Big Ollie by his colleagues on the Eight-Three. (He was not so affectionately called *Fat* Ollie by various despicable types he had busted over the years.) Big/ Fat Ollie was both fat *and* big. He also sweated a lot. And he smelled. Hawes considered him a pig.

'Looks like he was beat to death, don't it to you ?' Ollie asked.

'Yeah,' Hawes said.

They were climbing the steps to the first floor of the building, where the offices of Arthur Kendall, Attorney at Law, were located. Ollie was just ahead of Hawes, puffing up the stairs, a powerful aroma wafting back down the stairwell.

'Not with fists, though,' Ollie said, panting.

'No,' Hawes said.

'Sawed-off stickball bat,' Ollie said. 'Or maybe a hammer.'

'Medical examiner'll tell us,' Hawes said, and took out his handkerchief and blew his nose.

'You getting a cold there?' Ollie asked.

'No,' Hawes said.

'Summer colds are the worst kind,' Ollie said. 'You know this guy Kendall?'

'No,' Hawes said.

'He's a jig lawyer, represents half the punks who get in trouble around here.'

'Who represents the other half?' Hawes asked.

'Huh?' Ollie said, and opened the door to Kendall's office.

Kendall's secretary looked up from her desk in surprise. She was perhaps twenty-three years old, a good-looking black girl wearing an Afro cut, a pale blue jumper over a white blouse, her legs bare, her pastel-blue pumps off her feet and resting to the side of her swivel chair. Her surprise seemed genuine enough, but Hawes wondered how she could possibly have missed all the excitement downstairs – a dead man lying on the floor of the lobby, radio motor patrol cars at the curb, the police photographer taking pictures, the assistant medical examiner bustling about, the ambulance waiting to carry the body to the morgue.

'Yes?' she said, and bent over to put on her shoes.

'Detective Weeks,' Ollie said, '83rd Squad.'

'Yes?' the girl said.

'What's your name?' Ollie asked.

'Susan Coleridge.'

'We got a dead man downstairs,' Ollie said.

'Yes, I know,' Susan answered.

'Hear anything happening down there?' Ollie asked.

'No.'

'How come? It's just down one flight of steps there.'

'I was typing,' Susan said. 'And the radio was on.'

'It ain't on now,' Ollie said.

'I turned it off when I heard the police cars. I went out in the hall to see what was happening. That's when I realized Charlie'd been killed.'

'Oh, you knew him?'

'Yes. He worked upstairs.'

'Where?'

'Diamondback Development.'

'Your boss in?'

'He's in court.'

'Keeping you busy these days?' Ollie asked.

'Yes,' Susan said.

'So you didn't see nor hear nothing, is that right?'

'That's right,' Susan said.

'Thanks,' Ollie said, and motioned for Hawes to follow him out. In the hallway, Ollie said, 'These jigs *never* see nor hear nothin'. This whole neighborhood's deaf, dumb, and blind.'

'If she was typing . . .'

'Yeah, they're *always* typing,' Ollie said. 'Or the radio's on. Or the washing machine. Or something. It's always something. These jigs stick together like peanut butter and jelly. Nothing they like better than to see us busting our asses.' They had reached the second-floor landing now. The lettering on the frosted glass door at the top of the steps read DIAMONDBACK DEVELOPMENT, INC. Ollie glanced at it sourly, said, 'Sounds like a bullshit operation,' and pushed open the door.

Two black men in shirt sleeves were sitting at a long table near the windows. One of the men was tall and thin, light-complected, with a rather long nose and mild amber eyes. The other was quite dark, a heavy-set man with brown eyes magnified by thick-lensed glasses. He was chewing on the stub of a dead cigar. The wall to the left of the table was hung with large photographic blowups of rows and rows of tenements, alongside of which were pinned architectural drawings for what looked like a city of the future. Half a dozen of the buildings in the blowups had large red X's taped across their faces. The tabletop was covered with eight-by-ten glossies of tenements and empty lots. The heavy-set man was holding a stack of photographs of gasoline stations and putting them on the table, one by one, before the amber-eyed man, who then consulted a typewritten sheet. Both of them looked up together as Ollie walked briskly toward the table.

'Detective Weeks,' he said in his abrupt, direct manner. 'This is Detective Hawes. Who're you?'

'Alfred Allen Chase,' the amber-eyed man said.

'Robinson Worthy,' the man with the glasses said, and put down the gasoline-station pictures and shifted the dead cigar stub to the opposite side of his mouth.

'I'm investigating the murder of Charles Harrod,' Ollie said. 'I understand he worked here.'

'Yes, that's right,' Chase said.

'You don't seem too broken up over his untimely demise,' Ollie said. 'Business as usual, huh?'

'We've already called his mother, and we tried to reach his girl friend,' Chase said. 'What else would you like us to do? He's dead. Ain't nothing we can do about that.'

'What kind of job did he have here?'

'He took pictures for us,' Worthy said, and gestured toward the wall of tenement photographs and then the glossies on the desk.

'Just went around taking pictures of old buildings, huh?' Ollie said.

'We're a development company,' Chase said. 'We're trying to reclaim this whole area.'

'Sounds like a big job,' Ollie said in mock appreciation.

'It is,' Worthy said flatly.

'How much of it have you reclaimed so far?' Ollie said.

'We're just starting.'

'How do you start reclaiming a shithole like Diamondback?' Ollie said.

'Well, I don't know as it's incumbent upon us to explain our operation to you,' Worthy said.

'No, it ain't incumbent at all,' Ollie said. 'How long've you been in business here?'

81

'Close to a year.'

'You sure you ain't running a numbers drop?'

'We're sure,' Chase said.

'This is just a nice legit operation, huh?'

'That's what it is,' Worthy said. 'We're trying to make Diamondback a decent place to live.'

'Ah, yes, ain't we all,' Ollie said, imitating W. C. Fields. 'Ain't we all.'

'And we're trying to make a buck besides,' Chase said. 'Ain't nothing wrong with the black man making a buck, is there?'

'Don't bleed on me about the black man,' Ollie said. 'I ain't interested. I got a black man laying on the floor downstairs, and chances are he was done in by *another* black man, and all I know is that black men give me trouble. If you're so goddamn beautiful, how about starting to *act* beautiful?'

'Reclaiming the area is a legal, responsible, and proud enterprise,' Worthy said with dignity. 'Charles Harrod worked for us on a part-time basis. We have no idea why he was killed or who killed him. His murder in no way reflects on what we're trying to do here.'

'Well put, Professor,' Ollie said.

'If you're finished,' Worthy said, 'we've got work to do.' He picked up the glossy photographs of the gasoline stations, turned to Chase, and said, 'This one is on Ainsley and Thirty-first. Have you . . .'

Ollie suddenly reached over, clamped one hand into Worthy's shirt front, yanked him out of his chair, and slammed him against the wall of tenement blowups and architectural drawings. 'Don't get wise with me,' he said, 'or I'll ram those gas stations clear down your throat, you hear me?'

'Cut it out, Ollie,' Hawes said.

'You keep out of this,' Ollie said. 'You hear me, Mr Robinson Worthy, or do you hear me?'

'Yes, I hear you,' Worthy said.

'What'd Harrod *really* do for this bullshit operation?'

'He took pictures of abandoned tenements which we . . .'

'Don't give me any crap about your development company. You and your friend here probably got records as long as . . .'

'That is not true,' Worthy said.

'Shut up till I'm finished talking,' Ollie said.

'Let go of him,' Hawes said.

'Go on home,' Ollie said over his shoulder. His fist was still clamped into Worthy's shirt front, and he was still holding him pinned to the wall like one of his own architectural drawings. 'The stiff downstairs is mine, and I'll handle this any way I want to.'

'I'll give you thirty seconds to turn him loose,' Hawes said. 'After that, I'm calling in to file departmental charges.'

'Charges?' Ollie said. '*What* charges? This man is running a phony bullshit operation here, and he's scared to death I'm going to find out just what he's covering. Ain't that right, Mr Robinson Worthy?'

'No, that's not right,' Worthy said.

Hawes walked slowly and deliberately to the telephone on one corner of the desk. He lifted the receiver, dialed Frederick 7–8024, and said, 'Dave, this is Cotton Hawes. We've got a police officer manhandling a witness here – unnecessary use of force and abuse of authority. Let me talk to the lieutenant, please.'

'Whose side are you on, anyway?' Ollie said, but he released Worthy's shirt front. 'Put up the phone, I was just having a little fun. Mr Worthy knows I was just kidding around. Don't you, Mr Worthy?'

'No, I don't,' Worthy said.

'Put up the phone,' Ollie said.

Hawes replaced the phone on its cradle.

'Sure,' Ollie said. He sniffed once, tucked his shirt back into his trousers where it had ridden up over his belt, and then walked to the door. 'I'll be back, Mr Worthy,' he said. 'Soon as I find out a little more about this company here. See you, huh?' He waved to Hawes and walked out.

'You okay?' Hawes asked Worthy.

'I'm fine.'

'Were you telling the truth? Did Charlie Harrod *really* take pictures for you?'

'That's what he did,' Worthy said. 'We're looking for buildings that've been abandoned. Once we find them, we do title searches and then try to locate the landlords – which isn't always an easy job. If we can get to them before the city repossesses a building . . .' Worthy paused. In explanation, he said, 'If a building's been abandoned, you see, the landlord stops paying taxes on it, and the city can foreclose.'

'Yes, I know that,' Hawes said.

'What the city does then is offer the building to any city agency that might want to use it. If none of them want it, the city offers it for sale at public auction. They have seven or eight of these auctions every year, usually at one of the big hotels downtown. Trouble is, you get into a bidding situation then, and so we try to find the landlord before it comes to that.'

'What do you do when you find him?' Hawes asked.

'We offer to take the building off his hands. Pay the back taxes for him, give him a little cash besides, to sweeten the pot and make it worth his while. Usually, he's delighted to go along. You've got to remember that he *abandoned* the building in the first place.'

'What do you use for capital?' Hawes asked.

'We're privately financed. There are black men in Diamondback with money to invest in projects such as this. The return they expect on an investment is only slightly more than we would pay a bank for interest on a loan.'

'Then why not go to a bank?'

'We've been to every bank in the city,' Chase said.

'None of them seem too enthusiastic about the possibility of developing property in Diamondback.'

'How many buildings have you bought so far?'

'Eight or ten,' Worthy said. He gestured toward the wall again. 'Those marked with the red crosses there, plus several others.'

'Did Harrod find those buildings for you?'

'*Find* them? What do you mean?'

'I take it he served as a scout. When he saw a building that looked abandoned . . .'

'No, no,' Chase said. 'We *told* him which buildings to photograph. Buildings we already knew were abandoned.'

'Why'd you want pictures of them?'

'Well, for various reasons. Our investors will often want to *see* the buildings we hope to acquire. It's much easier to show them photographs than to accompany them all over Diamondback. And, of course, our architects need photographs for their development studies. Some of these buildings are beyond renovation.'

'Who are your architects?'

'A firm called Design Associates. Here in Diamondback.'

'Black men,' Chase said.

'This is a black project,' Worthy said. 'That doesn't make it racist, if that's what you're thinking.'

'Did Harrod take these gas-station pictures, too?'

'Yes,' Worthy said. 'That's another project.'

'An allied project,' Chase said.

'How long was he working for you?'

'Since we started.'

'About a year?'

'More or less.'

'Know anything about his personal life?'

'Not much. His mother lives alone in a building off The Stem. Charlie was living with a girl named Elizabeth Benjamin, over on Kruger Street. She's been up here once or twice. In fact, she called him while he was here today.'

'What was he doing here?'

'We gave him a list of some buildings we wanted photographed.'

'What time was this?'

'He got here about eleven or so, stayed maybe a half-hour.'

'What about the girl?' Hawes said. 'Is she a hooker?'

Worthy hesitated. 'I couldn't say for sure. She's very cheap-looking, but that doesn't mean much nowadays.'

'What'd you pay Harrod for taking these pictures?'

'We paid him by the hour.'

'How much?'

'Three dollars. Plus expenses.'

'Expenses?'

'For the film. And for developing and printing it. And for

the enlargements you see here on the wall. Charlie did all that himself. He was very good.'

'But you say he worked only part time.'

'Yes.'

'How much would you say he earned in a week?'

'On the average? Fifty dollars.'

'How'd he manage to drive a Cadillac and wear hand-tailored suits on fifty bucks a week?' Hawes asked.

'I have no idea,' Worthy said.

7

Maybe Elizabeth Benjamin had some ideas.

Maybe Detective Oliver Weeks, in his desire to pin something on Worthy and Chase, had rushed back to the Eight-Three and was at this very moment searching through his files and calling the Identification Section, instead of being where he *should* have been, which was at 1512 Kruger, in Apartment 6A, shaking down the joint and finding out what Elizabeth knew about Harrod's source of income.

She was coming out of the apartment as Hawes approached the sixth-floor landing. She was wearing the clothes he had seen her in earlier, her high-stepping street clothes, and she was carrying two matched valises, one of which she put down on the floor. She pulled the door shut behind her, and was reaching for the valise when Hawes stepped onto the landing and said, 'Going someplace, Liz?'

'Yeah,' she said. 'Clear the hell out of this city.'

'Not yet,' he said. 'We've got something to talk about.'

'Like what?'

'Like a dead man named Charlie Harrod.'

'Reason I'm getting out of this city,' Elizabeth said, 'is because I don't want nobody talking about a dead *girl* named *me*. Now you mind getting out of my way, please?'

'Unlock the door, Liz,' Hawes said. 'We're going back inside.'

Elizabeth sighed, put down both valises, swung her shoulder bag onto her abdomen, unclasped it, and was reaching into it when she saw the revolver appear in Hawes's fist. Her eyes opened wide.

'Bring your hand out slowly,' Hawes said. 'Wide open and palm up.'

'I was only going for the key, man,' Elizabeth said, and withdrew her hand and turned the open palm toward Hawes, the key to the apartment resting on it.

'Turn the bag over,' Hawes said. 'Empty it on the floor.'

'Ain't nothing deadly in it.'

'Empty it, anyway.'

Elizabeth turned the bag over. As she had promised, there was nothing deadly in it. Hawes felt a trifle foolish, but no more foolish than he would have felt if she'd later pulled a .22.

'Okay?' she said, and began putting the collection of lipsticks, mascara, Kleenex, Life Savers, address book, wallet, loose change, ballpoint pen, postage stamps, and grocery list back into the bag. 'What'd you expect to find in there?' she said. 'An arsenal?'

'Just hurry it up,' Hawes said, still mildly embarrassed.

'No, tell me what you thought was in there, Officer,' she said sweetly. 'A squadron of B-52's?' She snapped the bag shut, threw it over her shoulder, and then turned to unlock the door.

'The whole Sixth Fleet?' she said, and threw the door wide and picked up the valises.

Hawes followed her into the kitchen, closing and locking the door behind them. Elizabeth put both bags down, went directly to the sink, leaned against it, and folded her arms across her breasts.

'You forgot to turn on the water tap,' Hawes said.

'Hell with it,' Elizabeth said. 'I don't care *what* they hear no more.'

'*Is* the place bugged?'

'From top to bottom. Can't even go to the john without somebody listening.'

'What about the phone?'

'Charlie busted the mike they had in there.'

'Who's bugging the place, Liz?'

'You got me.'

'What was Charlie into?'

'Photography.'

'What else?'

'That's all.'

'Are you a hooker?'

'No, Officer, I am not a hooker.'

'You're unemployed, right?'

'Right.'

'And Charlie was earning fifty dollars a week, right?'

'I guess so. I don't know what he earned.'

'Where'd he get the Cadillac?'

'He didn't say.'

'And the fancy threads?'

'Didn't say.'

'Have you ever been arrested, Liz?'

'Never in my life.'

'I can check.'

'So check.'

'Who're you running from, Liz?'

'I'm running from whoever killed Charlie.'

'Got any idea who that might be?'

'No.'

'Where's the bedroom?'

'What you got in *mind*?' Elizabeth asked, and grinned nastily.

'I want to look through Charlie's things.'

'His things've *been* looked through,' Elizabeth said. 'Four times already. The pigs've been in and out of this place like it was a subway station.'

'The police have been here before?'

'Not while we were home.'

'Then how do you know they were here?'

'Charlie set traps for them. Pigs ain't exactly bright, you know. Charlie found those bugs ten minutes after they planted them.'

'Then why didn't he rip them out?'

'He was jerking them off. He got a kick out of feeding them phony information.'

'About what?'

'About whatever they wanted to hear.'

'What did they want to hear, Liz?'

'Haven't the faintest,' she said.

'Why were the police interested in Charlie Harrod?'

'Who knows? He was an interesting person,' Elizabeth said, and shrugged.

'Was he your pimp?' Hawes asked.

'I ain't a hooker, so why would I need a pimp?'

'All right, show me the bedroom.'

'In there,' she said.

'Ladies first.'

'Yeah,' she said, and led him through the apartment.

There were two closets in the bedroom. The first one contained a dozen suits, two overcoats, three sports jackets, six pairs of shoes, two fedoras, and a ski parka. The labels in most of the suits, both overcoats, and one of the sports jackets were from a store specializing in expensive, hand-tailored men's clothing. Hawes closed the door and went to the second closet. It was locked.

'What's in here?' he asked.

'Search me,' Elizabeth said.

'Have you got a key for it?'

'Nope.'

'I'll have to kick it in,' Hawes said.

'You need a warrant for that, don't you?'

Hawes didn't bother answering. He backed away from the door, raised his right leg, and released it pistonlike and flat-footed against the lock. He had to kick it three more times before the lock sprang.

'I'm *sure* you need a warrant for that,' Elizabeth said.

Hawes opened the door. The closet wasn't a closet at all. Instead, it was a small room equipped as a darkroom, complete with steel developing tank, print washer, dryer, and enlarger. The room's single window was painted black, and a naked red safelight hung over a countertop that rested on a bank of low metal filing cabinets. The countertop was covered with eight-by-ten white-enamel trays, metal tongs, and packages of developer, hypo, and enlarging paper. Wires had been tacked from one wall to the other, hung with photography clips. Hawes tried all the file drawers under the counter, but they were locked.

'You wouldn't have the key to these, either, I suppose,' he said.

'I don't have the key to nothing but the front door,' Elizabeth said.

Hawes nodded and closed the door. The bedroom dresser was on the wall opposite the bed, alongside the single window in the room. He went through each drawer methodically, poking through Harrod's shirts and shorts, socks and handkerchiefs. In Harrod's jewelry box, tucked under three sets of long red underwear in the bottom drawer, he found eight pairs of cuff links, a wristwatch with a broken crystal, a high school graduation ring, four tie tacks, and a small key. He took the key out of the box and showed it to Elizabeth.

'Recognize it?' he asked.

'No.'

'Well, let's try it,' Hawes said, and went back into the darkroom. The key did not fit any of the file drawers. Sighing, Hawes went out to Harrod's dresser and replaced the key where he'd found it. With the girl following him, he went into the kitchen and carefully inspected the cabinet over the sink.

The bug, as he'd suspected, was tacked up under the bottom wooden trim. He followed the wire up to the molding where wall joined ceiling, and then across the room to the kitchen window. Stepping out onto the fire escape, he studied the rear brick wall. The wire ran clear up to the roof and then out of sight. He climbed back into the room again.

'The one in the john is behind the toilet tank,' Elizabeth said. 'There's another one in the bedroom, behind the picture of Jesus, and there's also one in the living-room floor lamp.'

'And you've got no idea who planted them?'

Elizabeth shrugged. Hawes went back to the cabinet and searched through the shelves. Then he went through the drawers in the cabinet flanking the sink, and the single drawer in the kitchen table.

He found the pistol in the refrigerator.

It was wrapped in aluminium foil, and it was hidden at the rear of the bottom shelf, behind a plastic container of leftover string beans.

The gun was a Smith & Wesson 9-mm Automatic. Tenting

his handkerchief over the butt, Hawes pulled out the magazine. There were six cartridges in the magazine, and he knew there would be one in the firing chamber.

'I don't suppose this belongs to you,' he said.

'Never saw it before in my life,' Elizabeth said.

'Just sprang up there among the string beans and celery, huh?' Hawes said.

'Looks that way.'

'Happen to have a license for it?'

'I just told you it's not mine.'

'Is it Charlie's?'

'I don't know whose it is.'

Hawes nodded, shoved the magazine back into the butt, tagged the gun, wrapped it, and stuck it into his jacket pocket. He gave Elizabeth a receipt for it, and then wrote his name and the squadroom telephone number on a slip of paper and handed it to her. 'If you remember anything about the gun,' he said, 'here's where you can reach me.'

'There's nothing to remember.'

'Take my number, anyway. I'll be back later,' he said. 'I suggest you stick around.'

'I've got other plans,' Elizabeth said.

'Suit yourself,' Hawes said, and hoped it sounded like a warning. He unlocked the door and left the apartment.

On the way down to the street, he wondered if he shouldn't have arrested her on the spot. The law sometimes puzzled him. He was now in possession of certain facts and certain pieces of evidence, but he wasn't sure any of them added up to grounds for a legal arrest:

1 Frank Reardon had been shot to death with two bullets from a 9-mm pistol.

2 Hawes had found a Smith & Wesson 9-mm pistol on the premises occupied jointly by Charles Harrod and Elizabeth Benjamin.

3 The gun had an eight-plus-one-shot capacity, but there were only seven bullets in it when he'd slid open the magazine for a look.

4 Harrod's name had been listed in Reardon's skimpy address book.

5 Barbara Loomis, the super's wife, had described as Reardon's visitors in the week or so before the fire a black man and a black girl who sounded a lot like Harrod and Elizabeth.

In other words, take this fellow Reardon. He's been seen socializing with two other people. He is found shot to death with a 9-mm pistol, and a 9-mm pistol is later found in the refrigerator of those very two people with whom he'd earlier been socializing. Pretty strong circumstantial stuff, huh?

But socializing is not a crime, and keeping a gun in your refrigerator doesn't necessarily mean you used it to kill someone, no matter *how* many bullets are in it. In fact, if you have a license for a gun, you can keep the gun in your refrigerator, your breadbox, or even your hat. It is not difficult to get a gun in the United States of America. People in America keep guns the way Englishmen keep pussycats. The reason people in America keep guns is because America is a pioneer nation, and one never knows when the Indians will attack. (Hawes knew, as a matter of absolute fact, that a band of fanatic Apaches in war paint had only the week before attacked an apartment building on Lakeshore Drive in Chicago.) That was why the National Rifle Association did all that lobbying in Congress – to make sure that pioneer Americans retained the right to bear arms against hostile Indians.

Elizabeth Benjamin and Charlie Harrod kept a gun in their refrigerator, so Hawes assumed they were at least as American as any Cherokee. But if an American had a license for a gun, carry or premises, you could not arrest him unless he committed a crime with the weapon. Until Ballistics told Hawes whether or not the suspect pistol was indeed the one that had chopped down old Frank Reardon, he did not have much he could pin on Elizabeth. He might be able to arrest her for keeping a gun without a premises permit, but she had claimed the gun was not hers, and the apartment she lived in was Charlie Harrod's, and he couldn't arrest Charlie for anything because Charlie was dead.

But even if the gun *did* turn out to be the murder weapon, Hawes had further doubts about arresting Elizabeth. If there was no way to link her to the pistol – no license, for example, no record of purchase, no fingerprints on it, nothing but the fact that she'd kept it in Charlie's icebox – what could they charge her with? The crime was murder, the biggest felony of them all. A party to a crime, according to the Penal Law, is either a principal or an accessory. If Elizabeth had directly committed the act of murder, or aided or abetted in its commission, whether present or absent, or directly or indirectly counseled, commanded, induced, or procured another to commit the murder, she was a principal. If, on the other hand, she had harbored, concealed, or aided the murderer after the commission of the crime, with intent that he might avoid or escape from arrest, trial, conviction, or punishment, having reasonable ground to believe that he had committed the crime – why then, she was an accessory. So what the hell was she? Hawes would have to ask the lieutenant. And assuming she was anything at *all*, principal *or* accessory, how could they prove it on the basis of a gun found in Charlie's refrigerator, even assuming it *was* the gun that had killed Reardon?

It sometimes got extremely difficult.

The joke about the patrolman chasing a fleeing bank robber, while simultaneously reading his regulations booklet in an attempt to discern whether or not he was permitted to fire his revolver, was too close to the truth for comfort. Hawes sighed and stepped out into the blazing heat of the afternoon, squinting his eyes against the onslaught of the sun.

There was always routine to fall back on.

Routine now dictated that he send the gun over to the Ballistics Section of the Police Laboratory with a *Rush-Urgent* request, and then run a Pistol Permits check on Harrod and the girl. Routine further dictated that he get somebody from the Safe and Loft Squad to open Harrod's file drawers. Or would he need a goddamn court order for that, too?

Sometimes he wished he worked in an office building, running an elevator.

*

Detective First Grade Michael O. Dorfsman worked for the Ballistics Section, and it was he who took the hurry-up call from Cotton Hawes. He was already in possession of the two spent 9-mm cartridge cases, as well as the pair of bullets dug from the head of Frank Reardon. One of those bullets had been slightly deformed through collision with bone, but the other, once buried deep in Reardon's brain matter, was in excellent condition. He had not yet begun work on the evidence, because the cartridge cases had been sent to him only yesterday, and the bullets had arrived this morning, sent to him from the morgue after the autopsy had been performed.

There were ways of determining the make of an unknown firearm by examination of the shell casings and bullets, and since Dorfsman was an expert, he undoubtedly would have discovered before long that the gun which had fired the 9-mm cartridges had been a Smith & Wesson 9-mm Automatic Pistol. But this would have involved a thorough search for marks on the cartridges, dismissing such insignificant marks as those left by the gun's guide lips or the magazine slide and concentrating instead on more characteristic marks. Then, too, Dorfsman might have examined the one bullet that was still in good condition and come up with a classification in terms of caliber, direction of rifling twist, and number of lands and grooves which would have eventually yielded the murder weapon's make – even without the corroborative cartridge evidence.

Hawes merely saved him a lot of time.

Hawes sent over a Smith & Wesson 9-mm Automatic Pistol, and now all Dorfsman had to do was compare the cartridges he had on hand with test cartridges fired from the suspect weapon, and lo and behold, he would know whether *this* gun was indeed *the* gun.

As simple as that.

Even Dorfsman's wife knew that the word 'automatic' as it applies to a handgun means, simply, that the introduction of a new cartridge into the firing chamber is accomplished by the weapon rather than the shooter. In other words, an automatic pistol is in reality a 'self-loading' pistol. When one cartridge is fired, another moves into place immediately, ready for subsequent firing, whereas a revolver needs to be cocked by the thumb or the tripper finger. Dorfsman's wife didn't much care to know that the action of an automatic pistol is what makes it possible to identify shells fired from such a pistol. Dorfsman, on the other hand, *had* to understand the action if he was to perform his job properly. And, as he had said to his wife on more than one occasion, 'This is where the action is, baby.'

1 You have a Smith & Wesson 9-mm automatic pistol.
2 You slide a magazine into the butt of your gun. The magazine contains eight cartridges. You slip an extra cartridge into the firing chamber, giving you a total capacity of nine shots. You are ready now for killing people, if that's your bag.
3 When you squeeze the trigger, the bullet comes out of the gun barrel and hits somebody in the head.
4 At the same time, the pistol's recoil forces the empty cartridge case back, and causes the barrel slide to retreat and to open, and the empty shell is ejected.
5 The slide, with a spring assist, moves back to its original forward position, and another cartridge moves up into the firing chamber, and the firing pin is ready once again, and if you squeeze the trigger yet another time, another bullet will come rushing out of the barrel.

Since all this action involves a number of movable parts, and since those parts are made of steel whereas shell casings are made of softer metals like copper or brass, the gun parts will leave marks on the cartridges. And since no two guns are exactly alike, no two guns will mark a cartridge in exactly the same way. That's what makes a Ballistics Section possible, and that's why Michael O. Dorfsman had a job.

The parts of the gun that mark a cartridge are:

1 The breechblock. That's the whatchamacallit on top of the gun, where the cartridge sits just before you pull the trigger to send the bullet zooming on its way. The breechblock has little ridges and scratches left by tools at the factory (tools, tools, capitalist tools!) and these in turn leave impressions on the cartridge.

2 The firing pin. That's the little sharp whozits there that hits the percussion cap when you squeeze the trigger, and causes an explosion of gasses that propel the bullet out of the metal cartridge case and down that old gun barrel and into somebody's head. The firing pin, naturally, leaves a mark where it strikes the percussion cap.

3 The extractor. That's the little mother-grabber there that recoils with the slide mechanism after a cartridge is fired, leaving marks in front of the shell rim.

4 The ejector. That's the dojigger there that throws the empty cartridge case out of the pistol and onto the floor where smart cops can find it and figure immediately that the gun used was an automatic since revolvers don't throw anything on the floor except people who happen to be standing in front of them when they go off. The ejector leaves marks on the head of the shell.

If you know the marks a gun can leave, and if you know where to look for them on a spent cartridge case, why then, all you have to do is fire some shells from the suspect gun, retrieve them, and mark them for identification. Then you take the shell found at the scene of the crime, and you also mark *that* for identification, since any normal Ballistics Section has a lot of loose shells around, and you don't want to spend all your time playing the shell game when you've got more important matters to consider – like homicide, for example. Then you wash (yes, that's right, *wash*) all the shells in your favorite detergent (a woman works from sun to sun, but a man's work is never done) and you are now ready to compare them. You do this with a microscope, of course, and you photograph your findings under oblique light to bring the marks into sharp relief, and then you paste up an enlargement of the suspect shell alongside an enlargement of the comparison shell, and you record the marks on each the way you would record the whorls and tents and loops and ridges of a fingerprint – and there you are.

Where you are, if you are Michael O. Dorfsman, is in that euphoric land known as Positive Identification. It is very nice when all those marks and scratches line up like separate halves of the same face. It makes a man feel good when he's able to pick up the telephone and call the investigating detective to report without question that the gun delivered to Ballistics was definitely the gun that fired the bullets that killed somebody.

Which is exactly what Dorfsman did late that Friday afternoon.

Cotton Hawes, in turn, felt as though he had just caught a pass hurled by the quarterback. All he had to do now was run it to the goal line. Pistol Permits had earlier reported that no license had been issued to either Charles Harrod or Elizabeth Benjamin to carry a handgun or to keep one on the premises. The last permit issued for the particular gun in question, a Smith & Wesson 9-mm Automatic Pistol bearing the serial number 41–911–R had been issued on October 12, 1962, to a man named Anthony Reed, then residing in Isola. A check of the telephone directories for all five sections of the city disclosed no listing for an Anthony Reed. But 1962 was a long time ago, and God knew how many hands that pistol had traveled through since Reed was issued his premises permit. A chat with the lieutenant had assured Hawes that since the pistol had been found in the refrigerator on the premises normally occupied by Elizabeth Benjamin, possession could be presumed to be hers, and if she didn't have a permit for it, they could nail her with a gun violation at the very least. In addition, if and when Ballistics came up with a positive make, Hawes could feel free to arrest Elizabeth as either a principal or an accessory to the crime of murder. Lieutenant Byrnes wasn't sure either charge would stick, but her arrest would give them an opportunity to question her legally. Hawes now had a green light from Ballistics, and he was ready to go uptown after Elizabeth. He was, in fact, putting on his jacket preparatory to leaving the squadroom when the telephone rang again. He picked up the receiver.

'87th Squad, Detective Hawes,' he said.

'Hawes, this is Ollie Weeks.'

'Hello, how are you?' Hawes said without noticeable enthusiasm.

'Listen, I'm sorry about that little fracas with the jigs,' Ollie said. 'I don't want you to get the idea I'm a cop who shoves people around.'

'Now where would I get that idea?' Hawes said.

'It's just that the whole operation up there looks like a phony to me, that's all,' Ollie said. 'I've been working all afternoon here, and I found out a few things about our friends Worthy and Chase. I ain't done yet, but in the meantime, I don't want you to get the wrong idea about me.' Ollie paused, apparently waiting for an answer. When he received none, he said, 'Also, I got the ME's report on Harrod, and I thought you might be interested. He was beat to death, like we figured.'

'What was the weapon? Did the report say?'

'A numerosity of weapons,' Ollie answered, imitating W. C. Fields. 'A veritable numerosity. Leastways, that's how the ME's got it figured. He says there were blunt instruments used and ...'

'Instruments? Plural?'

'Yeah, plural. More than one instrument. And also, there was a stab wound under Harrod's left arm, though that wasn't what killed him. The blows to his head killed him, and the ME's opinion is that the weapons used were of varying weights and sizes.'

'In other words, Harrod was attacked by more than one person.'

'It looks that way,' Ollie said. 'Also, the ME found lesions and scars on Harrod's arms and legs, and traces of heroin in the stomach, the parenchymatous organs ...'

'The what?'

'I don't know how to pronounce it,' Ollie said. 'I'm reading it here from the report. And also the brain. You probably know this already, but the ME tells me alkaloids disappear from the system in about twenty-four hours, so it's safe to assume Harrod had shot up sometime during the day. Also, there were white paint scrapings under the fingernails of his right hand.'

'Paint, did you say?'

'Yeah. Looks like Harrod was a photographer, a junkie, and

99

a house painter besides. Anyway, that's what I've got so far. I'm still checking on that operation Worthy and Chase are running up there, and I'll let you know if I come up with anything else. What's with you?'

'I was just on my way out to pick up Harrod's girl friend.'

'What for?'

'I found a gun in her icebox, and Ballistics just made it as the weapon used in this homicide we're investigating.'

'What homicide? You're not talking about Harrod, are you?'

'No, no.'

'Because he wasn't shot, you know. I already told you . . .'

'This is another homicide. There are wheels within wheels, Ollie.'

'Ah yes, ain't there always,' Ollie said, imitating W. C. Fields again. 'Ain't there always. You want me to come along?'

'I can handle it alone.'

'What are you charging her with?'

'Murder/One. It won't stick, but it might scare her into telling us what she knows.'

'Unless she stands firm on Miranda-Escobedo and tells you to go jump.'

'We'll have to see.'

'When will you be back there?'

'In an hour or so.'

'I'll come over,' Ollie said, accepting an invitation Hawes could not remember extending. 'I want to sit in on the questioning.'

Hawes said nothing.

'And listen,' Ollie said, 'I hope you don't think I was shoving that jig around because I enjoyed doing it.'

'I'm in a hurry,' Hawes said, and hung up.

He had reached the gate in the slatted railing when the phone rang again. Carella was down the hall in the men's room, and Hal Willis was in with the lieutenant. Hawes grimaced and picked up the receiver at the phone nearest the railing, '87th Squad, Hawes,' he said.

'Cotton, this is Dave downstairs. I got a hysterical lady on the line, wants to talk to you.'

'Who is she?'

'Elizabeth something. She can hardly talk straight, I didn't catch the last name.'

'Put her on,' Hawes said.

She came on the line in an instant. Her normally low-pitched voice was high and strident. 'Hawes?' she said. 'You better get here fast.'

'Where are you, Liz?'

'The apartment. I did what you said, I stayed here. And now they've come to get me.'

'Who?'

'The ones who killed Charlie. They're outside on the fire escape. They're gonna smash in here as soon as they work up the courage.'

'Who are they, Liz? Can you tell me that?'

He heard the sound of shattering glass. He heard a medley of voices then, and the piercing sound of Liz's scream before someone gently replaced the phone on its cradle. Hawes hung up, raced down the iron-runged steps to the muster room and told Dave Murchison, the desk sergeant, to call the dispatcher and have a car sent to 1512 Kruger Avenue, Apartment 6A, assault in progress. Then he ran outside to the curb and started his own car, and headed uptown.

8

It was close to six o'clock when Hawes got to Diamondback. Two radio motor patrol cars were parked at the curb in front of the building, their red dome lights rotating and blinking. Two patrolmen, one black and one white, were standing on the stoop looking out over the crowd of men and women who had gathered to enjoy another of the city's outdoor summer spectacles. A plainclothes cop with his shield pinned to the pocket of his jacket was sitting in one of the cars, the radio mike in his fist, the car door open, one foot outside on the curb. Hawes locked his car, and then pinned his own shield to his jacket as he walked across to the building. He climbed onto the stoop, identified himself to the nearest patrolman, and said, 'I called in the 10–34. What happened?'

'Lady upstairs is near dead,' the patrolman said. 'Ambulance is on the way.'

'Who's up there now?'

'Lewis and Ruggiero, from the other car, and a Detective Kissman of the Narcotics Squad. He's the one who got here first. Busted in the door, but whoever did the job was already gone. Must've been more than one of them. They messed her up real bad.'

'Who's that on the squawk box?'

'Detective Boyd, the Eight-Three.'

'Tell him I'll be upstairs, okay?' Hawes said, and went into the building.

He was stopped on the fifth floor by one of the patrolmen from the second r.m.p. car. He identified himself, and went up to the sixth floor. The patrolman outside 6A glanced at Hawes's shield and said nothing as he went into the apartment. Elizabeth was lying unconscious on the floor near the kitchen table. Her clothes were torn and bloodied, her jaw hung open, and both legs were twisted under her at an angle that clearly indicated they'd been broken. A man in a brown cardigan

sweater was sitting at the kitchen table, the telephone receiver
to his ear. He looked up as Hawes came in, waved, and then
said, into the mouthpiece, 'Got no idea. I busted in because
all hell was breaking loose.' He listened a moment, and then
said, 'All of it, from the phone call on. Right, I'll talk to you
later.' He hung up, rose, and walked toward Hawes, his hand
outstretched. He was a tall, angular man with a relaxed and
easy manner. Like the other policemen on the scene, he wore
his shield pinned to an outer garment – in his case, the left-
hand side of his sweater, just over the heart.

'I'm Martin Kissman,' he said. 'Narcotics.'

'Cotton Hawes, 87th,' Hawes said, and reached for Kissman's extended hand.

'Oh,' Kissman said, surprised. 'So *you're* Hawes, huh?'

'What do you mean?' Hawes said, puzzled.

'I was going to call you later today, soon as I got relieved.
We've got the apartment bugged, I've been sitting the wire.'

'Oh,' Hawes said. 'You got my message, huh?'

'Loud and clear. And I got the conversation you had with
her later, after Harrod was killed. They knew the joint was
wired, huh? I should have realized it. We thought the phone
mike went dead, but that didn't explain the waterfall whenever
anybody was talking in the kitchen. I told the lieutenant they'd
tipped, that the only time they said anything they didn't want
us to hear was in the kitchen. Everything else was either phony
leads or routine garbage, like where they planned to go that
night, or what they were buying for dinner. I also got some
very sexy tapes from the bedroom mike, if you know anybody
who's interested.' Kissman grinned, pulled a pipe and tobacco
pouch from the pocket of his sweater, and began filling the
pipe.

For the first time, Hawes noticed the holes burned in Kissman's sweater. Hawes's father had smoked a pipe, and there
were always burn holes in his sweater, not to mention the carpet, the furniture, and on several occasions the drapes. To
make matters worse, the Hawes family had owned a Siamese
cat with a penchant for eating wool. There had been no valid
excuse for that animal's appetite; she was not pregnant, she

had no vitamin deficiencies of which Hawes was aware, she was simply a voracious wool-eating beast. What the coals from his father's pipe did not accomplish, the cat did. Hawes's mother once said to his father, 'You look moth-eaten all the time.' His father had looked up in surprise and said, 'What do you mean, Abby?'

Hawes realized he was smiling only when Kissman, still loading the pipe, said. 'Something?'

'No, no,' Hawes said, and shook his head. 'Why's the place wired?' he asked.

'We knew Harrod was a junkie, and we suspected he was a pusher as well. We were trying to get a line on the big boys.'

'Any luck?'

'Not so far. Harrod sent us on wild-goose chases all over town. That's one of the reasons I figured he'd tipped to the bug. But the lieutenant said no, so who's going to argue with a lieutenant?'

Kissman struck a match and began puffing great clouds of smoke into the kitchen. Neither of the two men so much as glanced at the unconscious girl. They both knew an ambulance was on the way, and there was nothing they could do for Elizabeth right now – except try to discover who was responsible for her present condition. Besides, there is a curious detachment about police officers confronted with the results of bloody mayhem. Like surgeons performing an operation – the hole in the surgical sheet circumscribing the area of surgery, the rest of the body covered, the lung or the liver or the brain becoming a part somehow isolated from and unrelated to the whole – detectives will often dissociate the victim from the crime itself, throw a sheet over the body, so to speak, so that they can concentrate completely on the specific part requiring their full attention. Elizabeth Benjamin lay hurt and bleeding on the kitchen floor, and the ambulance was on the way, and now the detectives discussed the who's and why's and wherefore's with all the detachment of surgeons peering into an open heart.

'The first I heard of Harrod's murder,' Kissman said, 'was when I picked up the conversation with you and the girl earlier

104

today. You know what I thought? I thought, Great, there goes a lot of hard work up the chimney.'

'Were you listening when the girl called me later?'

'Picked it up on the bug there under the cabinet. Just *her* side of the conversation, you understand. Then I picked up the glass smashing, and I heard these guys busting in on her, and her screaming, and I rushed right over. I'm staked out in an apartment in the next building; we ran our wires up over the roof and then down the back side. Took me maybe five minutes to get here. I found the girl just the way she is. Whoever broke in had gone out again, probably the same way. At least, I didn't meet anybody coming down the stairs on my way up. The cars got here maybe two minutes after I did. You the one who sent them?'

'Yeah,' Hawes said. 'I didn't think I could . . .'

'There she is,' someone at the door said, and Hawes turned to see two ambulance attendants and what he assumed was an intern coming into the room.

The intern bent quickly over Elizabeth, his eyes darting from her bruised and bleeding face to the hanging jaw, over the ripped front of her jersey top and the purple marks on her exposed breasts, and then down to the obviously broken legs. The ambulance attendants put down their stretcher and lifted her gently onto it. Elizabeth moaned, and the intern said, 'It's all right, dear.' He was perhaps twenty-five years old, but he sounded like a man who'd been practicing medicine for sixty years. One of the attendants nodded to his partner, and they picked up the stretcher again.

'How does it look?' Kissman asked.

'Not so great,' the intern replied. 'If you want to check in later, I'm Dr Mendez, Diamondback Hospital.'

'Think we'll be able to talk to her?' Hawes asked.

'I doubt it, that jaw looks broken,' Mendez said. 'Give me a ring in an hour or so.' The attendants had already left the apartment. Mendez nodded curtly and followed them out.

'The girl said you'd been in here a few times,' Hawes said. 'Was she right?'

'Right as rain,' Kissman said. 'Came in six times altogether.'

'She said *four*.'

'Shows how careful we can be when we want to,' Kissman said. 'We were all playing a little footsie here. Harrod knew the place was bugged and gave us false leads, and we came in four times that we let him know about, but two *more* times without letting him know.'

'Find anything?'

'Nothing. Took off all the switchplates, searched the toilet tank, the bedsprings, the ceiling fixtures, you name it. Only place he could have hidden any dope was up his rear end.'

'How about those locked file cabinets in the darkroom?'

'What file cabinets?'

'Under the counter in there.'

'Those must be new.'

'When were you in here last?'

'About a month ago.'

'Let's bust them open now,' Hawes said.

'I'll see if the guys downstairs have a crowbar,' Kissman said, and went out.

Hawes walked over to the window. The glass had been completely smashed out and the box of geraniums had been overturned, the soil scattered over the windowsill, the uprooted flowers knocked into the room and onto the floor. Not four feet from the broken window, Elizabeth Benjamin's blood stained the linoleum. Hawes stared at the blood for a long while, and then went to the phone and dialed the squadroom.

Carella picked up on the third ring. 'Where the hell are you?' he said. 'I go down the hall for a minute, and the next thing I know you've vanished.'

'Didn't Dave fill you in?'

'Dave got relieved more than an hour ago. Nobody ever tells me anything,' Carella said.

'Somebody broke in on the Benjamin girl and roughed her up,' Hawes said. 'She was on the phone with me when it started. I ran right over. I found out who planted the wire up here, Steve. A guy named Kissman from Narcotics.'

'Right, I know him,' Carella said. 'Alan Kissman, right?'

'Martin Kissman.'

'Martin Kissman, right,' Carella said.

106

'Did I tell you Ollie Weeks called?'

'No.'

'You must've been down the hall. The ME told him Harrod was killed by several people armed with an assortment of weapons. He was a junkie, Steve.'

'Is that why Kissman had the place wired?'

'Right. We're going to bust into these locked file drawers as soon as he gets back with a crowbar. What's going on up there?'

'Nothing much. Nothing connected with this, anyway.'

'You think we should run our own check on Worthy and Chase?'

'What do you mean our *own* check? Who else is running one?'

'Ollie Weeks. I thought I told you that.'

'I must've been down the hall. What's your reasoning, Cotton?'

'My reasoning is if Harrod had tread marks running up and down both arms, his bosses should have noticed, especially in the summertime with short-sleeved shirts. But all they could tell me was that he took pictures for them. Maybe Ollie's right. Maybe the development company *is* a front.'

'For what?'

'Drugs? Kissman thinks Harrod was a pusher.'

'Even if he was, that doesn't mean Worthy and Chase knew anything about it.'

'Then why didn't they tell me he was a junkie? He'd just been killed. What were they protecting?'

'I don't know. But let Ollie do the digging for us. One thing we don't need right now is more work.'

'I don't like Ollie,' Hawes said.

'Neither do I, but . . .'

'Ollie's a bigot.'

'That's right, but so's Andy Parker.'

'Yeah, but I *have* to work with Parker, he's on the goddamn squad. I *don't* have to work with Ollie.'

'He's a thorough cop.'

'Hah!' Hawes said.

'He is. There's a difference between him and Parker.'

'I fail to see it.'

'There is. It's the difference between crab grass and dandelions. Parker is the crab grass, ugly as hell, and absolutely good for nothing. Ollie's the dandelion . . .'

'Some dandelion,' Hawes said.

'A dandelion,' Carella insisted. 'Just as ugly as the crab grass, except when it blooms a pretty yellow flower. And don't forget, you can put it in a salad.'

'I'd *like* to put Ollie in a salad,' Hawes said. 'And drown him with oil and vinegar.'

'Let him handle the legwork, Cotton. Did he say he'd be in touch?'

'He should be showing up at the squadroom any minute now. You know what I wish? I wish Artie Brown is there when he starts spewing some of his racial horse manure. Artie'll knock him on his ass and send him gift-wrapped to his uncle in Alabama.'

'Why's he coming up here?' Carella asked.

'He thinks I'm on my way in with Benjamin girl. Tell him what happened, will you? Maybe he'll go right back home and stick pins in his little Sidney Poitier doll.'

'How bad is the girl?'

'Pretty bad. Looks like they broke her jaw and both her legs.'

'Why?'

'I don't know. Here's Kissman now, I'll talk to you later. Are you heading home?'

'In a little while.'

'I think we'd better meet on this later tonight, Steve. It's getting complicated.'

'Yeah,' Carella said, and hung up.

*

There is hardly anything you can't open with a crowbar, except maybe a tin of anchovies.

Hawes, Kissman, and Detective Boyd of the Eight-Three utilized a sort of non-stop approach in prying open the locked drawers in Harrod's darkroom. Instead of prying one open, and then examining its contents, they opened the entire lot en masse, six drawers in all, and then sat down to examine the contents at their leisure. It took them ten minutes to open the drawers, and nearly an hour and ten minutes to go through the contents. Because the only light in the darkroom was furnished by the red bulb hanging over the counter, they carried all six drawers into the bedroom, and turned on the overhead fixture, and sat among and between the drawers like kids rummaging through old furniture and clothes in the attic of an old house on a rainy day. Outside, the street noises began to diminish – this was the dinner hour in Diamondback.

Charlie Harrod had been a busy person.

So had Elizabeth Benjamin.

Part of Harrod's busy-ness had to do with the taking of drugs. If there had been any doubts left by the medical examiner's report as to whether or not Charlie had been an addict, these all vanished when the detectives went through the contents of the first drawer. In an empty cigar box in that drawer, they found a hypodermic syringe, a teaspoon with the bottom of the bowl blackened and the handle bent, and half a dozen books of matches. Hidden in the barrel of a two-cell flashlight, they found three glassine bags of a powdery white substance they assumed to be heroin. In a second empty cigar box in that same drawer, and presumably kept as insurance against hard times, they found a safety pin, an eyedropper, and a sooty bottle cap fitted into a looped piece of copper wire. The bottle cap was a makeshift spoon, used to heat and dissolve the heroin with water; the safety pin was used for puncturing the vein; the eyedropper was used for injecting the drug into the bloodstream – very primitive, but very effective if the monkey was on your back and your syringe was broken and you'd run out of kitchen utensils.

Further back in the drawer they found a collection of books, pamphlets, and magazine and newspaper clippings relating to drugs and drug abuse, including one reprinted from the monthly police magazine to which most cops in the city subscribed. A separate manila folder contained a file of newspaper clippings reporting seizures of large shipments of heroin, arrests of pushers, police drives against the narcotics traffic, and what appeared to be a page Xeroxed from a text on toxicology, outlining the symptoms of alkaloid poisoning and its antidotes. There was nothing in the first drawer to indicate that Harrod had been dealing. The stash of heroin was minuscule, the amount an addict might normally keep on hand to avoid running short. Whereas the law in this city stated that possession of more than two ounces of heroin created rebuttable presumption of intent to sell, none of the detectives believed there was enough dope hidden in Harrod's flashlight to support such an allegation.

The remaining five drawers were packed with manila folders, labeled and cataloged alphabetically. From the way each of the separate manila folders was labeled, one might have suspected that the late Charlie Harrod's tastes had run to matters literary, theatrical, mythological, historical, linguistic, instructional, and religious. A sampling of the white labels pasted to the tabs on the folders revealed, for example, such diversified titles as SNOW WHITE AND THE SEVEN DWARFS, and LASSIE, and THE TROJAN WARS, and INFANT AND CHILD CARE, and THE GOLDEN FLEECE, and TARZAN OF THE APES, and THE JOYS OF YIDDISH, and ZOO STORY, and THE BERLITZ SELF-TEACHER (*French*), and WAR AND PEACE, and THE RISE AND FALL OF THE THIRD REICH, and even the HOLY BIBLE. One look at the contents of the folders, however, revealed what the titles really meant, and showed besides that Charlie Harrod had possessed a certain perverse sense of humor.

The folders contained photographs.

Some of the photographs were obviously recent and had probably been taken by Charlie himself, here in his own apartment – in the bedroom primarily, but also in the living room, the kitchen, and (in one remarkable series) on the fire escape outside. Some of the photographs were enlarged prints of pictures taken decades ago – the costumes identifying the separate eras, telltale cracks, rips and fade marks indicating sources other than Charlie's own camera.

All of the photographs were pornographic.

They depicted every conceivable sex act ever committed, devised, or imagined by and for humans and animals of every age, color, stripe, or persuasion in duets, trios, quartets, quintets, sextets (of course), crowds, mobs, tribes, or (as it seemed in one of the pictures) entire nations – performed with or without restraints, mechanical appliances, tools, gadgets, instruments of torture, or benefit of clergy. Since all of the photographs were marked with price tags, it was reasonable to assume that Charlie had been something more than a casual collector. In fact, it was almost mandatory to assume that Charlie's expensive clothes and automobile were direct residuals of his penchant for photography. An important part of his busyness then (or business, if you prefer) was the peddling of porn. Nor had Elizabeth Benjamin been lying when she'd stated she was not a hooker. Elizabeth Benjamin was a photographer's model. At least two-thirds of the pictures in Charlie's gallery featured Elizabeth as performer in a variety of roles. Her repertoire was apparently unlimited, her poses unselfconscious and unabashed, her star quality evident.

And so the dinner hour passed pleasantly, and dusk settled on the city as Kissman, Boyd, and Hawes spent a quiet interlude looking at dirty pictures, each man knowing at last what it felt like to be a member of a censorship board who, compelled to read all sorts of filthy books in the service of the community, finally determines which of those are too vile to be permitted space on the shelves of the public library.

The experience was purifying.

*

Steve Carella was beginning to feel like an accountant.

It was now twenty minutes to eight, and Ollie Weeks had arrived at the squadroom almost two hours ago with quite a bit of information on the firm called Diamondback Development, Inc., run by two gentlemen named Robinson Worthy and Alfred Allen Chase. Ollie had apparently done some thorough digging since the time he'd left Worthy and Chase with a promise to look into their company operations and the time he'd phoned Hawes to say, 'I found out a few things about our friends Worthy and Chase,' a choice bit of meiosis, if ever there'd been one. Actually, Ollie had done some fine and fancy

111

footwork in those few hours before most business offices closed for the day, proof positive that fat men are light on their feet and good dancers besides.

He had, of course, been running his case by the book, and the book dictated that certain things be done as a matter of form in the investigation of a suspect business operation. Ollie had done them all, and he was now anxious to prove to Hawes (or to Carella as his substitute) that he had not been overly hasty in his judgment of the men who ran Diamondback Development. He knew Carella from a case they had worked jointly some five years back, at which time Carella had called Ollie on his peculiar idiosyncrasy of referring to an eighty-six-year-old Puerto Rican matriarch, grandmother to twelve children, and proud parent of a son who was then running for the City Council, as 'that decrepit spic twat'. Ollie had taken offense at Carella's having taken offense, and the working relationship had been somewhat strained from that moment on. Neither of the two men exchanged too many pleasantries now as they got down to business. Carella had a homicide, and Ollie had a homicide, and the two homicides were maybe linked somehow, and that gave them something in common.

'This is what I found out about those two creeps,' Ollie said. 'First thing I did was call Cartwright and Fields, the credit reporting agency downtown, and talked to a lady named Mrs Clara Tresore of the Service Department. She gave me a lot of static about coming down to the fourth floor there and showing my credentials, and I told her it was already three in the afternoon and I didn't have time to come running downtown. So she hemmed and hawed, and finally called me back a half-hour later to give me the information I needed. Okay, it turns out that Diamondback Development was incorporated in September of last year, the three officers of the corporation being Robinson Worthy as president, Alfred Allen Chase as vice-president, and a guy named Oscar Hemmings as treasurer. Principal assets at the time of incorporation were $5,975, stock divided evenly between the three officers. Principal business activity of the firm was stated to be "the purchase and redevelopment of properties in that section of the city known as Diamondback". Sounds legit so far, don't it?'

'It does,' Carella said. He was beginning to think about Roger Grimm and his import business, and the firms in Hamburg and Bremerhaven. He immediately put them out of his mind. He even had trouble explaining the new math to his twins, and he suspected he was not cut out for an executive position in an international cartel. He did not yet know that in a little while Hawes would bring him information about yet another business, the little porn shop Charlie Harrod had been running. His mind would have snapped.

'You with me so far?' Ollie asked.

'I'm with you,' Carella said, not entirely sure he was.

'Okay, I next checked with the Better Business Bureau *and* the Credit Bureau of Greater Isola *and* also the Diamondback Credit Bureau, and I learned that these guys have good credit ratings, no complaints from anybody they ever dealt with, bills paid on time, all the rest of it. It still looks good, it still looks legit.'

'When does it start looking bad?' Carella asked.

'Give me a minute, will you?' Ollie said. He consulted his notes, which he had fastidiously hand-lettered onto the backs of several printed Detective Division forms, and then looked up again. 'Okay, so these guys are in the business of buying property and redeveloping it, right? So I called Land Transfer Records, and I found out these guys bought a total of nine abandoned buildings in Diamondback since they went into business. They bought all those buildings from their original owners, and the prices paid were less than what they would've got them for at auction. You want to hear some of the prices?'

'Sure, why not?' Carella said.

'The prices are important,' Ollie said. 'For example, they paid $6,300 for a three-story brick building on the south side of Thorp Avenue; $2,700 for a two-story frame on Kosinsky Boulevard; $3,800 for a three-story limestone façade on Hull and Twenty-fifth, and like that. Total cost for the nine buildings was $48,750. You got that?'

'I've got it,' Carella said, not so sure he had.

'So next I called License & Building Records, and I learned that Diamondback Development, even though they now have nine buildings that they own outright and a firm of architects making drawings for them, has only renovated *one* building in all this time – a dump over on St Sebastian Avenue. The architects are a firm called Design Associates on Ainsley. I called them and they told me their fee for the drawings had been $50,000.'

'How'd you know who the architects were?'

'I called Worthy and Chase and they told me, how do you think? Those two creeps are anxious to establish they're legit; they told me the name of their architects, and also the name of their bank – which was their first mistake.'

'What's the bank?'

'Bankers First on Culver Avenue, three blocks from their office. I called about four o'clock, it must've been. They close the doors at three, you know, but they keep working inside there till five, sometimes six o'clock. I spoke to the manager, a guy named Fred Epstein, and he told me Diamondback Development had a checking account and also a safety deposit box. I asked him if I could take a peek in the box, and he said not without a court order – you need a goddamn court order for a coffee break nowadays. So I ran out of the office, and downtown, and I got a municipal judge to write me the order, and I got uptown again around five and went through the box, and guess what?'

'What?' Carella said.

'There's close to $800,000 in cash in that box. Now that's a pretty hefty sum for three bare-assed developers who started their business with $5,975, don't you think?'

'I think so, yes.'

'And who, don't forget, have already laid out close to a hundred thousand buying buildings and getting architects to make drawings for them. Not to mention what it must've cost to do that one renovation job. Where'd all that money come from, Carella?'

'I don't know,' Carella said.

'Neither do I.'

'Did you tell all this to Hawes?'

'I knew it when I called him, but there was one other thing I wanted to check before I filled him in.'

'What was that?'

'The third guy in Diamondback Development. Oscar Hemmings. The treasurer.'

'Did you get a line on him?'

'Yeah, he lives in that building on St Sebastian, the one Diamondback Development renovated. I plan to look him up tomorrow. I already checked with the IS, he hasn't got a record. Neither has Worthy, by the way. Chase is another story. He took a fall five years ago, for Burglary/Two, was sentenced to ten at Castleview, got out on parole in three-and-a-half.'

'When was that?'

'When he was released? Be two years come November.'

'Has the FBI got anything on any of them?'

'Got a request in now,' Ollie said. 'I should be hearing pretty soon.'

'You've been busy, Ollie,' Carella said. He did not like Ollie, but he made no attempt to hide his admiration for what Ollie had accomplished in the space of several hours. This was what he had tried to explain to Hawes earlier. Fat Ollie Weeks was a terrible person, but in many respects a good cop. Throwing away his investigative instincts and his dogged ferreting-out of facts would be tantamount to throwing away the baby with the bath water. And yet, working with him rankled. So what was one to do? In all good conscience, what was one to do? Treat him like a computer spewing out information, thereby dehumanizing him and committing the same offense that so offended? Ollie Weeks was a problem. Moreover, Carella suspected he was a problem without a solution. He was what he was. There was no taking him aside and calmly explaining the facts of life to him. 'Uh, Ollie baby, it's not *nice*, these things you say. Some people may find them offensive, you dig, Ollie?' How do you explain to a crocodile that it's not nice to eat other animals? 'It's in my nature,' he'll reply. 'That's why God gave me such sharp teeth.' God alone knew why He had given Ollie Weeks such sharp teeth, but short of knocking them out of his mouth, Carella didn't know quite what to do about them.

'You're damn *right* I've been busy.' Ollie said, and grinned, thereby adding modesty to all his other virtues.

Both men heard voices in the corridor outside, and turned toward the slatted railing. Hawes was coming into the squad-room, followed by Kissman, who was carrying a tape recorder. Kissman looked older than Carella remembered him. He suddenly wondered if he looked the same way to Kissman.

'Hi, Alan,' he said.

'Martin,' Kissman said.

'Martin, Martin, right,' Carella said, and nodded. He was tired, his head was full of too many figures. Money, money, money, it always got down to love or money in the crime business. 'This is Ollie Weeks of the Eight-Three. Martin Kissman, Narcotics.'

The men shook hands briefly, and looked each other over, like advertising executives wondering if they'd be working together on the same account.

'Where's the girl?' Ollie asked, suddenly realizing Hawes had gone out to bust Elizabeth Benjamin and had come back with a Narcotics cop instead.

'In Diamondback Hospital,' Hawes said.

'With two broken legs, some broken ribs, and a broken jaw,' Kissman said.

'Why didn't you call me?' Ollie said to Hawes, offended.

'It all happened too fast,' Hawes answered. 'But Kissman's got a tape of what went on in the apartment . . .'

'A tape?' Ollie said. He was enormously confused. He blinked his eyes and reached for a handkerchief. Mopping his brow, he said, 'I don't know what's going on here,' which was true enough.

Hawes explained it to him while Kissman set up the recorder. Then the four men sat in straight-backed chairs around the desk as Kissman pressed the PLAY button. The tape started with a sequence that had been recorded earlier in the day:

His things've been *looked through. Four times already. The pigs've been in and out of this place like it was a subway station.*

'Who's that?' Ollie whispered.

'The girl,' Hawes whispered back.

The police have been here before?

Not while we were home.

Then how do you know they were here?

'Who's the guy?' Ollie asked.

'Me,' Hawes said.

'You?' Ollie said, even more confused.

Charlie set traps for them. Pigs ain't exactly bright, you know. Charlie found those bugs—

'Can you run it ahead?' Hawes asked.

—ten minutes after they planted them.

Kissman stopped the tape, and then pressed the FAST FOR-WARD button, watching the footage meter, stabbing the STOP button, and then pushing the PLAY button again. This time he was closer on target:

—better get here fast. The apartment. I did what you said, I stayed here. And now they've come to get me. The ones who killed Charlie. They're outside on the fire escape. They're gonna smash in here as soon as they work up the courage.

There was the sound of shattering glass, and then at least three, possibly four different voices erupted onto the tape:

Get away from that phone!

Hold her, watch it!

She's . . .

I've got her!

Elizabeth screamed. There was a click on the tape, probably the phone being replaced on its cradle, and then the sounds of a scuffle, a chair being overturned perhaps, feet moving in rapid confusion over the linoleum floor. From the squadroom railing, Meyer Meyer, coming back with a container of coffee and a cheese Danish, said, 'What's going on?'

'Quiet,' Hawes said.

Elizabeth was sobbing now. There were the sodden sounds of something hard hitting human flesh.

Oh, please, no.

Shut up, bitch!

Hold her, get her legs!
Please, please.

She screamed again, a long blood-curdling scream that raised the hackles on the necks of five experienced detectives who had seen and heard almost everything in the horror department. There was the sound of more blows, even in cadence now, a methodical beating being administered to a girl already unconscious.

Come on, that's enough.
Hold her, lay off, you're gonna kill her!
Let's go, let's go.
What's that?
Let's get the hell out *of here, man.*

There was the sound of footsteps running, the tinkle of glass, window shards probably breaking loose as they went out through the window. The sensitive mike picked up a moan from the kitchen floor, and then there was utter silence.

Kissman turned off the recorder.

'How many do you think?' Hawes asked.

'Four or five,' Ollie said. 'Hard to tell.'

'There's something I don't understand,' Carella said, frowning. 'You want to run that back for me, Martin?'

'To where?'

'To where one of them says something about killing her.'

Kissman rewound the tape, and then pushed the PLAY button:

Oh, please, no.
Shut up, bitch!
Hold her, get her legs!
Please, please.

The girl's terrified scream sounded into the squadroom again, and again the men sat speechless, like children who did not know about monsters in the night. They listened again to the speechlessly administered beating, and waited for the next voice on the tape:

Come on, that's enough.
Hold her, lay off, you're gonna kill her!
Let's go, let's go.

'Cut it there,' Carella said, and Kissman turned off the machine. 'I don't get those instructions.'

'What instructions?'

'The guy tells somebody to hold her and to lay off at the same time,' Carella said. 'That doesn't make sense.'

'He keeps yelling that all through the tape,' Kissman said.

'What do you mean?'

'To hold her. He keeps telling one of the other guys to hold her.'

'There's a lot of noise on that tape,' Ollie said. 'Maybe we're hearing it wrong.'

'No, that comes through loud and clear,' Hawes said. 'He yells "Hold her," there's no question about it.'

'Do they sound young to you?' Kissman said.

'Some of them.'

'They sound *black*, that's for sure,' Ollie said, and Hawes frowned at him, but Ollie didn't seem to notice.

'Play that part again, will you?' Carella said. 'About killing her.'

Kissman located the spot on the tape, and they played the single sentence over and over again, listening to it intently, searching for meaning in the seeming contradiction: Hold her, lay off, you're gonna kill her! Hold her, lay off, you're gonna kill her! Hold her, lay off, you're gonna kill her! Hold her, hold her, hold 'er, hold 'er, holder, holder ...

'It's his *name*!' Hawes said, rising suddenly out of his chair.

'What?' Ollie said.

'Holder! Jamie Holder!'

*

Three of them went into the clubroom together – Ollie Weeks because officially the Harrod homicide was his; Carella and Hawes because officially the Reardon homicide was theirs. Besides, it does not hurt to have a lot of firepower when you're going in against an indeterminate number of hoodlums.

The clubroom was in the basement of a tenement on North Twenty-seventh Street. They had no difficulty locating the clubroom because the cops of the 83rd kept an active file on all neighborhood street gangs, and a call from Ollie to his own squadroom immediately pinpointed the headquarters of The Ancient Skulls. Standing in the basement corridor outside the clubroom, they listened at the door and heard music within, and several voices, male and female. They did not knock, they did not bother with any formalities; they were dealing here with people who had maybe committed murder and assault. Fat Ollie kicked in the door, and Carella and Hawes fanned into the room directly behind him, guns drawn. Two young men standing at the record player turned toward the door as it burst open into the room. A boy and a girl, necking on a sofa on the wall opposite the door, jumped to their feet the moment the detectives entered. Two other couples were dancing close in separate dim corners. They turned immediately toward the intruders and stopped dancing, but did not break apart. There was another door at the far end of the room. Ollie moved to it swiftly and kicked it open. A naked boy and girl were on the bed.

'Up!' Ollie said. 'Put your clothes on!'

'What is this?' one of the boys near the record player asked.

Hawes recognized him as the bearded pool player named Avery Evans.

'It's a bust,' Carella said. 'Shut up.'

'Where's Jamie Holder?' Hawes asked.

'In the other room.'

'Hurry it up, Lover Boy,' Ollie said. 'Man outside wants to talk to you.'

'What'd *I* do?' Holder asked from the other room.

'I'm the president here,' Avery said, moving away from the record player. 'I'd like to know what's going on, if you don't mind.'

'What's your name?' Carella said.

'Avery Evans.'

'Nice to meet you,' Ollie said. 'You! Get over against the wall there! This ain't a Friday night social. Cut off that record player!'

'I expect you have a warrant,' Avery said.

'Yeah, here's our warrant,' Ollie said, and gestured with the .38 Special in his fist. 'You want to read it?'

'I don't understand this,' Avery said. 'The Ancient Skulls have always cooperated with the police. Would you mind telling me . . . ?'

'We'll tell you at the squadroom,' Ollie said. 'Come on, girls, you too!' He shoved his pistol into the other room, and shouted, 'You ain't dressing for the governor's ball, Holder! Shake it up in there or I'll come help you.'

The girl who had been in bed with Holder had dressed rapidly, and now came out of the other room, buttoning her blouse. She could not have been older than sixteen, a doe-eyed girl with a beautiful face and a flawless complexion.

Avery stepped up close to Carella and said, as if he were confiding to him, 'I suppose you realize that The Ancient Skulls are the only neighborhood club that . . .'

'Tell us later,' Carella said.

'Will you tell us why you're taking us to the squadroom?' Avery asked. 'Has there been some trouble with one of the other clubs?'

'No,' Carella said flatly.

Jamie Holder came into the room. He was as big as Hawes remembered him, with powerful wrists and huge hands. 'What's the static, man?' he asked.

'They've made a mistake, Holder,' Avery said.

'Oh, sure,' Holder said.

*

The Ancient Skulls were not all as old as their title proclaimed, but they nonetheless ranged in age from eighteen to twenty-six, which meant that they were not juvenile offenders and could therefore be questioned in a police station. Nobody had ever told the cops in this city exactly *where* a juvenile offender *should* be interrogated. Usually, they took any suspect juvenile to a part of the building that was not contaminated by various and sundry sordid types, thereby giving lip service to the ruling – strange are the ways of the Law. The Ancient Skulls, of course, were entitled to a recitation and explanation of their rights, and they were entitled to maintain silence if they so chose, and they were also entitled to legal counsel whether or not they decided to answer any questions. Miranda-Escobedo, the Supreme Court decision that granted all these rights, was not the hindrance some police officers claimed it to be. In fact, a survey among law-enforcement officers around the country had revealed that as many confessions had been obtained *since* the Miranda-Escobedo decision as before, *without* the use of back-room, third-degree techniques.

Avery Evans, the leader of The Ancient Skulls, was the oldest member of the gang, twenty-six going on twenty-seven. He was also the smartest, and presumably the toughest. He maintained that the police were making some kind of mistake, and he said he would freely answer any and all questions they asked him. He had nothing to hide. The Ancient Skulls had always cooperated with the police, and he was certainly willing to cooperate with them now. He advised the other members of the gang – or at least those members present, it being estimated that there were a hundred and twelve Ancient Skulls residing in Isola and another fifty-some-odd in Riverhead – that they, likewise, could answer any questions the cops put to them. Avery Evans was cool, smart, tough, supremely confident, and the leader of a proud and noble band. He did not know, of course, that the police had a tape recording of what he and his proud and noble followers had done to Elizabeth Benjamin.

'You still haven't told me what this is all about, man,' he said.

He was sitting in the Interrogation Room at the 83rd, at a long table facing a one-way mirror, sometimes called a two-way mirror – stranger and *stranger* are the ways of the Law. Those cops who called it a one-way mirror did so on the grounds that it only reflected on *one* side, whereas the other side was a clear pane of glass through which you could observe the person looking into the mirror. One way you looked *into* it, one way you looked *through* it – hence a one-way mirror. But there were other cops who called it a two-way mirror because of its double role as looking-glass and glass-for-looking. You could not reasonably expect cops, who couldn't even agree on the interpretation of Miranda-Escobedo after all these years, to agree on what the hell to call a one-way-two-way mirror. The important thing was that any suspect looking into the mirror, which hung conspicuously on the wall of the otherwise bare-walled Interrogation Room, knew immediately that he was looking into a trick mirror and (nine times out of ten) being photographed through it from the adjacent room. Which is just what was happening to Avery Evans, with his complete knowledge. But, of course, he had nothing to hide. He was convinced the cops had nothing on him. Let them take his picture through their phony mirror, let them run through all the nonsense. In half an hour he'd be back dancing at the old clubhouse.

Ollie – who was running the interrogation, since this was his corral, so to speak, even though it differed only slightly in decrepitude from the squadroom of the 87th – immediately said, 'Before we start, let me make sure again that you understand your rights as we explained them to you, and that you're willing to answer questions without a lawyer here. Is that right?'

'Oh, sure, sure,' Avery said. 'I got nothing to hide, man.'

'Okay, then, you want to give me your full name?'

'Avery Moses Evans.'

'Where do you live, Ave?'

'On Ainsley Avenue – 1194 Ainsley, Apartment 32.'

'Live alone?'

'I live with my mother.'

'What's her name?'

'Eloise Evans.'

'Father living?'

'They're separated,' Avery said.

'Where were you born, Ave?'

'Right here. This city.'

'How old are you?'

'I'll be twenty-seven two days before Christmas.'

'Where do you work?'

'I am at present unemployed.'

'Are you a member of the gang called The Ancient Skulls?'

'It's a club,' Avery said.

'Sure. Are you a member?'

'I'm the president,' Avery said.

'Is Jamie Holder a member?'

'Jamison Holder, that's right. Good man,' Avery said, and grinned.

'Where were you and Jamie Holder tonight between five and five-thirty PM?'

'I don't remember exactly.'

'Try to remember exactly,' Ollie said.

'Hanging around.'

'Hanging around where?'

'Probably shooting pool.'

'Where would that have been?'

'Ace Billiards. On Kruger Street.'

'Anybody see you and Jamie at that time?'

'Lots of guys from the Skulls were there.'

'Anybody besides members of your gang?'

'Club.'

'Anybody besides them?'

'I couldn't say for sure. I don't make a habit of finding out who's in a place.'

'Know anybody named Charlie Harrod?' Ollie asked, and tweaked his nose with his thumb and forefinger. This was the signal to begin a flanking attack, Ollie continuing the frontal assault while Carella and Hawes closed in from either side.

'Never heard of him,' Avery said.

'Elizabeth Benjamin?' Hawes asked. 'Ever hear of her?'

'Nope.'

'Harrod was a junkie,' Carella said.

'Yeah?' Avery said, and smiled. 'I notice you used the past tense, man. Did he kick the habit?'

'Yes, he kicked it,' Hawes said.

'Good for him. We got no junkies in our club. I think you guys already know that. Ask any of the cops up here, they'll tell you the Skulls are clean.'

'Oh yeah, we know that,' Ollie said.

'It's a fact, man.'

'But you never heard of Harrod, huh?'

'Nope. All I know is if he kicked the habit, I'm proud of him. Too *much* junk in this neighborhood. That's one thing you got to say about the Skulls, we're doing our share to make this neighborhood a better place to live in.'

'Oh, ain't we all,' Ollie said, doing his now-famous W. C. Fields imitation, 'ain't we all.'

'And another thing,' Avery said, 'it's the Skulls, and *only* the Skulls, who're always negotiating with the other clubs to keep the peace around here. If it wasn't for us, you guys would have your hands full. There'd be war all the goddamn time. I think you owe us at least a *little* gratitude for that.'

'Oh, sure we do,' Ollie said.

None of the cops bothered to mention that if there were no street gangs, there would be no wars, and therefore no need for any of the gangs to negotiate for peace. Each of the men questioning Avery knew that today's gangs were far more dangerous than those existing twenty years ago, mainly because the current version came fully equipped with an ideology. The ideology provided a built-in justification for mayhem. If you're doing something because it's helping the neighborhood, why then, you can do any damn thing you like. Moreover, you can do it with a sense of pride.

'Where were you this afternoon, a little before twelve?' Hawes asked.

'Man, you guys sure expect a person to pinpoint his whereabouts, don't you?'

'You don't have to answer if you don't want to,' Hawes said.

'I got nothing to hide,' Avery said. 'I was probably down at the clubhouse.'

'Anybody see you there?'

'Oh sure, lots of the guys . . .'

'*Besides* members of the gang.'

'Only club members are allowed in the clubhouse.'

'By the clubhouse, do you mean the basement we found you in tonight?' Ollie asked.

'That's the clubhouse,' Avery said.

The three detectives had moved closer to him, and they now formed a somewhat claustrophobic circle around his chair. They began to interrogate him more rapidly now, firing their questions one after the other, Avery at first turning to look at each of them in turn, and then finally directing all of his answers to Ollie, who stood directly in front of him.

'You got an annex to that clubhouse?' Ollie asked.

'No.'

'Where do you keep your arsenal?' Carella asked.

'We don't have no arsenal, man. We're a peace-loving club.'

'No guns?' Hawes asked.

'No knives?' Carella asked.

'No ball bats?' Ollie asked.

'None of that stuff.'

'You wouldn't keep a stash of guns someplace else, huh?'

'No.'

'Someplace other than the clubhouse?'

'No.'

'Or knives?'

'No.'

'Charlie Harrod was stabbed today.'

'Didn't know him.'

'He was also beaten to death.'

'Still don't know him.'

'You familiar with that Kruger Street area?'

'Just a bit.'

'You just told us you shoot pool in Ace Billiards.'

'That's right, I do. Every now and then.'

'That's next door to where Charlie lived.'

'That a fact?'

'Apartment 6A, 1512 Kruger.'

'What about it?'

'Ever *in* that apartment?'

'Never.'

'Ever see Elizabeth Benjamin in the neighborhood?'

'Nope.'

'Did you know Charlie Harrod was a junkie?'

'Didn't know *what* he was. Didn't *know* the man, you dig?'

'Ever beat up a junkie?'

'Never.'

'That's a lie,' Ollie said. 'We had you punks in here six

months ago for beating up a pusher named Shoemouth Ken dricks.'

'That was a *pusher*, man. That wasn't no junkie. Junkies are sick people. Pushers are what *makes* them sick.' Avery paused. 'How come *you* know about that, anyway? You weren't the cop who handled it.'

Ollie reached behind him, lifted a manila folder from the desk, and threw it into Avery's lap. 'This is the file on your little club, Mr President. It gets thicker every day. We know all about you punks, and we know you stink.'

'Well now, I wouldn't say exactly that, Mr Weeks,' Avery said, and grinned, and handed the folder back to Ollie.

'We know, for example,' Ollie said, 'that you keep your arsenal in the apartment of one Melissa Beam at 211 North Twenty-third, and that it consists of fourteen handguns, two dozen hand grenades, six World War II bayonets and sheaths, and any number of switchblades, baseball bats, and sawed-off broom handles.'

'That's a lie, man,' Avery said. 'Who told you that jive?'

'A member of another little club called The Royal Savages.'

'*Those* jerks?' Avery said disdainfully. 'They wouldn't know an arsenal from their own assholes. Anyway, if you thought all that stuff was over there on Twenty-third, how come you didn't raid it?'

'Because the last time you were up here, Mr President, you made all kinds of law-abiding promises to a detective named Thomas Boyd, and in return he made a deal not to hassle you or your club.'

'That's right, we *are* law-abiding,' Avery said. 'We keep the peace.'

'Detective Boyd is over on Twenty-third right this minute,' Ollie said, 'busting into that apartment. I hope he doesn't find any weapons we can trace back to you and your gang. Like, for example, the knife that was used on Charlie Harrod.'

'He won't, don't worry,' Avery said, but he seemed a trifle shaken now. He cleared his throat.

'What do you call Jamie Holder?' Carella said.

127

'I call him Holder.'

'You call him by his last name?'

'That's right.'

'How come?'

'Jamie sounds like a pansy. He likes being called Holder. It's a strong name. He's a big man, and a proud man. Holder fits him good.'

'Ever hear of voice prints?' Hawes asked.

'Nope.'

'They're like fingerprints,' Carella said.

'We can compare them. We can make positive identifications of voices.'

'Ain't that interesting,' Avery said.

'We've got *your* voice on tape,' Ollie said.

'You been taping this?' Avery said, and looked quickly around for a hidden recorder. 'I didn't give you permission to do that.'

'No, no, we haven't taped this,' Ollie said, and smiled.

'We've got a tape, though,' Carella said, and smiled.

'You and Holder are the stars on it,' Hawes said, and smiled. 'Want to hear it, Avery?'

'Sure, why not?' Avery said, and shrugged, and folded his arms across his chest.

Ollie immediately left the squadroom. The tape recorder was in the Clerical Office down the hall, and he could have picked it up in thirty seconds flat, but he dallied for a full five minutes before returning to where Avery was sitting in his straight-backed chair, arms folded. Neither of the other two detectives had said a word to him while Ollie was gone. Now Ollie put the recorder on the desk, gave Avery a sympathetic look that translated as 'Man, are you in trouble,' and stabbed at the PLAY button. Casually, the detectives stood around Avery Evans and watched him as he listened to the tape.

Hawes? You better get here fast. The apartment. I did what you said, I stayed here. And now they've come to get me. The ones who killed Charlie. They're outside on the fire escape. They're gonna smash in here as soon as they work up the courage.

Avery blinked when he heard the sound of glass shattering. His arms still folded across his chest, he leaned forward only slightly when he heard the next voices:

Get away from that phone!

Holder, watch it!

She's . . .

I've got her!

Elizabeth screamed, and Avery began to sweat. The perspiration popped out on his forehead and ran down over his temples and cheeks as he heard the click of the phone being replaced on its cradle, the sounds of the chair being overturned, the tattoo of feet on linoleum, Elizabeth sobbing, the brutal sounds of flesh yielding to weapons.

Oh, please, no.

Shut up, bitch!

Holder, get her legs!

Please, please.

There was another scream, and the sweat rolled over Avery's jaw and into his beard, moved inexorably in rivulets down the corded muscles of his neck and was sopped up by the white T-shirt under the blue denim gang jacket. He listened to the beating, blinked when he heard the voices again:

Come on, that's enough.

Holder, lay off, you're gonna kill her!

Let's go, let's go.

What's that?

Let's get the hell out of here, man.

He listened to the running footsteps and the tinkle of the broken window shards, and turned his head away when Elizabeth moaned. The tape went silent.

Ollie cut off the machine. 'Recognize any of those voices?'

Avery did not answer.

'The girl's alive,' Hawes said. 'She'll identify you.'

'How come you didn't finish her off? Figure a scare was good enough?'

Avery did not answer.

'Did you think Harrod was a pusher?'

'Did his expensive clothes and Caddy fool you?'

'Did you think the girl was dealing, too?'

Avery still said nothing.

'Who hung up the phone, Ave?'

'We'll get fingerprints from the receiver, you know.'

'And we'll compare the voices on that tape with voice prints of you and Holder.'

'And the *rest* of your pals, too.'

'And we'll compare the white paint scrapings under Harrod's fingernails with the paint on those jackets you wear.'

'How many of you jumped Harrod?'

'You stupid little punk!' Ollie shouted. 'You think you can run around killing and hurting anybody you want? We're gonna lock you up and throw away the key, you hear me, Mr President?'

'I want a lawyer,' Avery said.

9

It was still Friday. It had been Friday forever.

Legal Aid sent over an attorney to make certain that none of The Ancient Skulls' rights were being violated. At the same time the detectives – figuring they had hooked into real meat – called the District Attorney's office and asked that a man be sent over before they messed up the legal ramifications by asking any further questions. By eleven PM everyone was assembled. By ten minutes to twelve they all realized they were going to get nowhere, since the Skulls' appointed attorney advised them to keep silent. The man from the DA's office felt they had a good case, nonetheless, and so the Skulls were booked for acting in concert on one count of homicide and one count of assault, and were taken downstairs to the detention cells to await transportation to the Criminal Courts Building for arraignment. The lawyers shook hands with each other and the detectives, and everybody left the squadroom at a few minutes past midnight. It was Saturday at last. Ollie Weeks had cracked his case in less than twelve hours, and one might have expected him to go home and sleep the sleep of angels secure in the knowledge that he had performed admirably and well.

Carella's bedside phone rang in the middle of the night. He fumbled for the receiver, lifted it, and said, 'Hullo,' not sure he was talking into the right end.

'Carella? This is Ollie Weeks.'

'Ollie?' Carella said. 'Oh, hullo, Ollie. How are you? What time is it, Ollie?'

'I don't know what time it is,' Ollie said. 'Carella, I can't sleep.'

'That's too bad,' Carella said, and squinted at the luminous dial on the alarm clock near his bed. It was ten minutes past four. 'Have you tried counting sheep, Ollie?'

'I've been thinking about this guy,' Ollie said.

'What guy, Ollie?'

'This guy Oscar Hemmings. The third guy in Diamondback Development.'

'Oh, yes,' Carella said. 'Yes, what about him?'

'I've been thinking if I wait till morning, he's liable to be not there.'

'Well,' Carella said, and hesitated. It seemed to him that Ollie had just uttered a choice *non sequitur*, but he couldn't be quite certain because he was still half asleep.

'At his apartment, I mean,' Ollie said. 'At the address I have for him.'

'Yes, there's always the chance he'll be out,' Carella said, and looked at the clock again.

'Unless I go there *now*,' Ollie said.

'It's four o'clock in the morning,' Carella said. 'It's twelve past four.'

'That's the idea,' Ollie said. 'Nobody's not home at four in the morning. It's too late to be out on the town and too early to be getting out of bed. If I go there now, I'm sure to nab him.'

'Okay,' Carella said. 'Fine.'

'What do you mean?'

'Go there. Go nab him.'

'You want to come with me?' Ollie said.

'No,' Carella said.

'Aw, come on.'

'No,' Carella said. 'Listen, are you crazy or something, waking me up at four o'clock, four-fifteen, whatever the hell it is? What's the matter with you? You cracked your case, you've got your . . .'

'Those guys up there bother me.'

'Why?'

'Because they've got $800,000 in their safety deposit box. Where'd those jigs get money like that if it ain't dirty money?'

'I don't *know* where, Ollie.'

'Ain't you even interested? Harrod worked for them, and Harrod knew Reardon, and Reardon is dead, and Hawes tells me Harrod's gun killed him. Now ain't that interesting to you?'

'It's interesting. But Harrod's *also* dead, and I can't arrest a dead man for killing another dead man.'

'Why are all these guys getting knocked off?' Ollie said.

'The homicides aren't connected,' Carella said patiently. 'You've *got* the punks who killed Harrod, and if Harrod killed Reardon, it was because Reardon knew about an arson in which Harrod may or may not have been . . . *Damn* it, Ollie, you're waking me up! I don't want to wake up! I want to go back to sleep. Goodnight, Ollie.'

Carella hung up. Beside him, his wife Teddy lay asleep with one leg twisted in the sheet. She *could* not, and therefore *had* not, heard the ringing telephone or the ensuing conversation, and for that he was grateful. He untangled the sheet, and was snuggling up close to her when the phone rang again. He snapped the receiver from its cradle and shouted, '*Yes*, damn it!'

'Steve?'

'Who's *this*?'

'It's me. Cotton.'

'What do you want, Cotton?'

'Did Ollie Weeks just call you?'

'Yes, Ollie Weeks just called me! And now *you're* just calling me! Why don't you two guys get married and stop bothering me in the middle of the goddamn night? I'm trying to sleep here. I'm trying to get some sleep here. I'm trying . . .'

'Steve?'

'What?'

'You want to go with him?'

'No, I don't want to go with him.'

'I think we ought to go with him,' Hawes said.

'You like him so much, *you* go with him,' Carella said.

'I don't like him at all, but I think maybe he's right,' Hawes said. 'I think maybe Diamondback Development has something to do with Roger Grimm's fires, and I think we're not going to get anything out of Worthy and Chase right now, but maybe we've got a chance to get something out of the third guy if we go up there in the middle of the night and surprise him. I think Ollie's right.'

There was silence on the line.

'Steve?' Hawes said.

There was more silence.

'Steve?'

'Where do you want to meet?' Carella said wearily.

*

They met in an all-night diner on Ainsley Avenue at a quarter to five. They sat in a corner booth and quietly discussed their next move. What they were about to do was risky in that they did not have a court order to enter the premises occupied by one Oscar Hemmings at 1137 St Sebastian, and if Hemmings so chose, he could tell them to run along and go play cops and robbers elsewhere. America was not yet a police state, and the Gestapo could not break down your door in the middle of the night and haul you out of bed. They could question Hemmings, true, because they were seeking information about a crime of which they had knowledge, but they couldn't question him unless he agreed to being questioned. If he refused, they could tell him they'd be back with a subpoena and he could answer questions before a grand jury, the choice was his, and that might scare him into cooperating. But they didn't want to go that route with Hemmings, and so they concocted a ruse in the diner, and they hoped the ruse would work. If he bought their story, he might talk to them and reveal something important. If he did not buy it, he was within his rights to slam the door in their faces.

The ruse they concocted was a good one and a simple one.

They assumed that Hemmings, being a partner in Diamondback Development, already knew that Charlie Harrod was dead. However, no matter how fast the Diamondback grapevine worked, he probably did not yet know that The Ancient Skulls had been picked up and charged with Harrod's murder. The several assumptions they had made about Roger Grimm's warehouse fire were that (a) Reardon had doped the booze the night watchmen later drank, and (b) Reardon had been killed because he might talk about his role in the arson. They knew, in addition, that Reardon had been visited two or three times in the week or so before the fire by two black men – one of whom had been Charlie Harrod; that Reardon had deposited $5,000 into his savings account five *days* before the fire; and that Elizabeth Benjamin had spent the two nights preceding the fire in Reardon's apartment, presumably to add a little sexual persuasion to the financial inducement he'd already received. A positive identification of Harrod and Elizabeth would have to be made by Barbara Loomis, who had seen them both. In the meantime, her descriptions seemed to jibe, and so they worked on the assumption that Reardon was the connecting link between Harrod and the warehouse fire.

What they wanted to know, and this was why they were visiting Hemmings in the early hours of the morning, was *why* Harrod had been involved in arson. Assuming he had contacted Reardon to engage his services in helping to administer the Mickey, and assuming Reardon had been paid $5,000 for those services, and assuming Elizabeth had been sent to him to sweeten the pot – why had Harrod wanted to burn down Grimm's warehouse in the first place? What was his motive? Was he working for Diamondback Development or for himself? Worthy and Chase had already said all they would ever say about Charlie Harrod. Good photographer, mother lives alone, girl friend a bit flashy, blah, blah, blah. Hemmings hadn't yet told them anything, and now they hoped he would – *if* their little ruse worked.

This was the structure upon which they based their plan:

Hemmings knew that Harrod had been killed.

Hemmings did *not* know The Skulls had been charged with Harrod's murder.

Worthy and Chase knew both Ollie and Hawes.

Worthy and Chase had undoubtedly told their partner, Hemmings, about the visit from the two cops, and may have also described them.

The only cop Worthy, Chase, and Hemmings did *not* know was Steve Carella.

This was the scenario they evolved:

Ollie and Hawes would knock on Hemmings' door. They would apologize for awakening him so early in the morning but they had a man with them who, they suspected, had killed

135

Charlie Harrod that afternoon. They would then produce the man, in handcuffs. The man would be rather tall and slender, with brown hair and brown, slanted eyes, an altogether unimpressive nebish, but nobody says you have to look like John Wayne in order to be capable of committing murder. The man in handcuffs would be Steve Carella.

Ollie and Hawes would tell Hemmings that the man, whose name they decided would be Alphonse Di Bari (over Carella's objections, since he didn't think he looked particularly Italian), had claimed he would never have murdered Charlie Harrod, because he was a close friend of his and had, in fact, worked together with him at Diamondback Development. It was essential to the case they had against Di Bari that someone from Diamondback Development either positively identify him as an employee, or else put the lie to rest. Hemmings, of course, would say he had never before seen this Alphonse Di Bari (Carella *still* objected to the name, this time on the grounds that he didn't particularly look like an Alphonse). Then the detectives would get sort of chummy with Hemmings and explain how they had tracked Di Bari to his apartment and found the murder weapon there, and Carella (as Di Bari) would protest all along that they had the wrong man, and would beg Hemmings to please tell these guys he legitimately worked for Diamondback Development, that Charlie Harrod had hired him to take photographs of a warehouse belonging to a man named Roger Grimm, *please*, mister, will you please tell these guys they're making a mistake?

Everybody would be watching Hemmings very closely at this point, hoping he would by his manner or by his speech drop something revealing (like perhaps his teeth) the moment the warehouse was mentioned. If he did not react immediately, they would keep hammering at the warehouse story, supposedly enlisting Hemmings' aid, listening all the while for telltale little clues, actually *questioning* him while making him believe they were in reality seeking information that would disprove Di Bari's lie.

It was not a bad scenario.

Listen, this was five o'clock in the morning, and they

weren't shooting a picture for Twentieth Century-Fox.

With Carella in handcuffs (he felt stupid), the detectives went into the building on St Sebastian Avenue and began climbing the steps to the fourth floor.

Even at this early hour of the morning, Ollie was no rose garden, but then again, he had never promised anybody he was. Cotton Hawes had a very sensitive nose. He hated firing his pistol senselessly because the stench of cordite almost always made him slightly nauseous. During his naval career this had been a severe handicap, since somebody or other always seemed to be firing a gun at somebody else or other. Ollie did not smell of cordite. It was difficult to place his smell.

'I thought they *renovated* this dump,' Ollie said. 'It's a garbage heap, that's what it is.'

Yes, Hawes thought, *that's* it.

They stopped outside Hemmings' door and knocked on it. And knocked on it again. And again, and again, and again. Nobody answered.

'What now?' Hawes asked.

'You think he's in there?' Ollie said.

'If he is, he's not letting us know about it.'

'He should be in there,' Ollie said, frowning. 'It's five o'clock in the morning. Nobody's not in bed at five o'clock in the morning.'

'Except me,' Carella said.

'What do you think?' Ollie said.

They held a brief consultation in the hallway outside Hemmings' door, and decided to call off the movie. They removed the handcuffs from Carella's wrists, and were starting down the steps to the street when Ollie said, 'What the hell are we pussyfooting around for?' and went back to the door and kicked it in without another word.

Carella and Hawes looked at each other. Hawes sighed. Together, they followed Ollie into the apartment.

'*Look* at this joint, willya?' Ollie said.

They were looking at it. They were, in fact, looking at it bug-eyed. For whereas 1137 St Sebastian was a tenement, and whereas the stairway leading up to the fourth floor had been as littered and as noisome as any to be found in the slums, and whereas the chipped and peeling door to Oscar Hemmings' apartment looked exactly like every other door on the floor, the apartment inside came as a series of surprises.

The first surprise was a small entrance foyer. You did not ordinarily find entrance foyers in Diamondback. Entrance foyers were for Marie Antoinette. In Diamondback, you stepped immediately into a kitchen. But here was an honest-to-God entrance foyer, with mirrors running around it on all three surrounding walls, optically enlarging the space and reflecting the images of three dumbfounded detectives. Ollie, who was already peeking past the foyer into the rest of the apartment, was thinking it resembled a place he had once seen on a science-fiction television show. Carella and Hawes, who were beside him, weren't thinking anything at the moment. They just stood there looking like a pair of baggy-pantsed Arabs who had accidentally wandered into a formal reception at the Israeli Embassy.

To the right of the entrance foyer was a kitchen, sleek with formica and walnut, brushed chrome, white vinyl tile. The thick pale blue carpet that began in the entrance foyer ran completely through the rest of the apartment. Knee-deep in it, or so it seemed, the detectives waded into the living room, where a lacquered white sectional couch nestled into the right-angle corner of the room, its cushions a deeper blue against drapes the color of the carpet. A huge modern painting, all slashes and streaks, red, blacks, whites, and varying shades of blue, hung over one section of the couch, illuminated by a pale white sculpted floor lamp operated from a mercury switch at the door. There was a walnut bar lined with glasses unmistakably designed in Scandinavia, glistening against a bottled backdrop of expensive whiskeys and liqueurs. Floor-to-ceiling walnut bookshelves covered the wall opposite one section of the couch, stacked with titles Ollie had meant to read but had never got around to.

A record turntable, a tape deck, an amplifier and a pair of

speakers at either end of the room comprised Hemmings' stereo system, and one long shelf on the bookcase wall contained at least two hundred long-playing albums and as many tape cartridges. At the far end of the room, serviced through a swinging door that led to the kitchen, was an oval walnut table with four chairs around it. A hanging buffet, waist-high, walnut and black formica, was on the wall behind the table. A second painting hung just above the buffet, positioned off-center, starkly abstract, repeating the color combinations of the larger painting across the room – red, black, white, and blue.

The bedroom was spartanly furnished, a low king-sized white lacquered bed with dark blue spread, pale blue carpet growing all around it, pale blue matching drapes at the window, a walnut dresser with a white formica top, a small, low easy chair upholstered in nubby black, a closet with slatted doors painted white and occupying the entire far wall of the room. The bathroom was entirely white. White tile, white fixtures, white shower curtain, white shag oval rug near the tub, white towels.

That was it. The apartment had most likely been composed of five rooms before the walls were knocked out and the space redivided. There were now three rooms and a bath, in addition to the small foyer. The renovation had undoubtedly cost Diamondback Development thousands and thousands of dollars.

'Nice,' Ollie said.

'Yeah,' Hawes said.

'Mmm,' Carella said.

Each man was thinking of his own salary.

'Let's check out the closets and drawers,' Hawes said.

They were starting for the bedroom again when Ollie stopped dead in his tracks. 'Somebody's coming,' he whispered. Neither Hawes nor Carella had heard a thing. They listened now, heard footsteps on the stairs outside, the clatter of high heels approaching the kicked-in entrance door. Ollie had

139

moved swiftly to the left of the door, and was standing against the mirrored wall, pistol drawn. He motioned Carella and Hawes to get out of sight.

In the hallway outside, they heard a small exclamation of surprise.

'Get in here,' Ollie snapped.

A girl stepped into the entrance foyer. She was a tall, attractive redhead, white, perhaps twenty-five years old. She was wearing a long green evening gown and green satin slippers, Cinderella returning from the ball at five in the morning to find the place full of burglars, or so it must have seemed to her. 'Take anything you want,' she said immediately, 'but don't hurt me.'

'We're police officers,' Ollie said, and the girl's mood and temperament changed at once.

'Then get the hell out of here,' she said. 'You've got no right breaking in here.'

'What's your name?' Ollie said.

'What's yours?' she answered.

'Detective First Grade Oliver Weeks, 83rd Squad,' he said, and holstered his gun and showed his identification. 'I *still* don't know your name.'

'Rosalie Waggener,' she said, and walked past the detectives and into the living room, stepping out of her shoes as she went and padding barefooted to the bar, where she immediately poured herself a brandy snifter full of Courvoisier.

'You live here, Rosalie?' Carella asked.

'I live here,' she said wearily, and tilted the snifter to her lips. Her eyes matched the color of the cognac in the glass.

'Does Oscar Hemmings live here?' Hawes said.

'No.'

'The apartment is listed in his name,' Ollie said.

'Where's it listed?' the girl asked.

'In the phone book.'

'That only means the *phone's* listed in his name. The apartment is mine.'

'Why'd you list the phone in his name?'

'Because a young girl living alone gets all kinds of phone calls.'

'Do *you* get all kinds of phone calls?' Ollie asked.

His question was transparent to Hawes and Carella – and to the girl as well. A pad like this in the heart of Diamondback spelled only one thing to the cops, and the girl knew exactly what they were thinking. But she chose to ignore the deeper meaning of the question. 'I don't get all kinds of phone calls because the phone is listed in Oscar's name,' she said simply, and sipped some more cognac.

'You live here alone?' Ollie asked.

'I do.'

'Been out tonight?'

'What do *you* think? I don't usually get dressed like this to bring in the milk.'

'Why *do* you get dressed like that?' Ollie asked.

Again, the question was transparent. And again, the girl chose to ignore its implications.

'I went to a party,' she said.

'Where?'

'On Silvermine Oval. Downtown.'

'What kind of party?'

'A private party.'

'Must've been a good party,' Hawes said.

'It was an excellent party,' Rosalie answered, and polished off the remainder of the cognac. Immediately, she poured herself another full snifter. 'Would you like to tell me what you're doing here?' she said.

'We're investigating an arson,' Carella said, deciding to play it at least partially straight; they were also investigating the business affairs of Diamondback Development, Inc.

'Tell us about Oscar Hemmings,' Ollie said.

'Oscar's not involved in any arson,' Rosalie said.

'Nobody said he was. Tell us about him.'

'He's a friend,' Rosalie said.

'Must be a very good friend, to let you list the phone in his name. You got a lease for this place?'

'I have.'

'Mind if I see it?'

'I don't keep it here.'

'Where *do* you keep it?'

'At my mother's house. In Riverhead,' she said quickly, and they knew immediately she was lying.

'Lease in your name?'

'Of course.'

'What'd it cost you to redecorate this place?'

'A lot.'

'How much?'

'I forget. I'm very bad on figures.'

'You must like living up here in Diamondback.'

'I like it fine.'

'Must've cost you thousands of dollars to fix up an apartment in one of the worst neighborhoods in the city,' Ollie said.

'Yeah, well, I like it here.'

'Got a lot of jig friends, have you?' Ollie asked.

'Listen, Ollie,' Hawes said, 'how about . . . ?'

'Black friends, do you mean?' Rosalie interrupted.

'That's what I said, ain't it?'

'Yes, I have some black friends.'

'You must have a lot of them, living in this neighborhood.'

'I have enough of them,' Rosalie said.

'White ones, too, I'll bet.'

'Yes, white ones, too.'

'You a call girl, Rosalie?'

'No.'

'Then what the hell are you doing in this place, huh? You want to tell us that?'

'I've already told you. I live here.'

'Where does Oscar live?'

'I don't know.'

'I thought you said he was a good friend. How come you don't know where he lives?'

'He recently moved.'

'From where?'

'He used to live up on the Hill. I don't know where he lives now.'

'When did you see him last?'

'Oh, must be two or three weeks, at least.'

'Let's take a look at some of your things, okay, Rosalie?'

'No, it's *not* okay,' she said.

'Rosalie,' Ollie said, slowly and softly and patiently, 'if you are running a whorehouse up here, we are going to hound your ass till we find out about it. Now how about cooperating? We're not trying to bust up the prostitution racket in this city. We're working on an arson.'

'I'm not a prostitute, and I don't care *what* you're working on.'

'No, you're just a Vassar graduate, right? Living here in Spadeland for the fun of it, right?'

'I can live where I like. There's no law against living wherever I want to live.'

'Correct,' Ollie said. 'Now tell us exactly where you were tonight.'

'Why?'

'Because all of a sudden this *has* become an investigation into illegal prostitution.'

Rosalie sighed.

'We're listening,' Ollie said.

'Go ahead,' she said, 'look through the place. I've got nothing to hide.'

Ollie and Hawes went into the bedroom. Rosalie poured herself another drink, and then said to Carella, 'You want some of this?'

'No, thank you.'

She sipped at the cognac, watching him over the rim of the glass. In the bedroom, Carella heard drawers being opened and closed. The girl grimaced and jerked her head toward the sound, trying to share with Carella her sense of outrage at this invasion of privacy. Carella gave no sign that he understood what she was trying to convey. The setup, to say the least, stank to high heaven; he, too, believed that Rosalie was a call girl.

143

Hawes came back into the living room. He was holding an American passport in his hands. 'This yours?' he asked.

'If you found it in my dresser, it's mine.'

Hawes opened the passport and began leafing through it. 'Travel a lot, Miss Waggener?' he asked.

'Every now and then.'

'Want to take a look at this, Steve?' he asked, and handed Carella the passport.

Carella studied the page to which it was opened. According to the stamped information on that page, Rosalie Waggener had entered West Germany through Bremen Flughafen on July 25, and had returned to the United States on July 27. Carella looked up from the passport. 'I see you've been to Germany lately,' he said conversationally.

'Yes.'

'How come?'

Ollie, who had been listening in the bedroom, said in imitation of an SS officer, 'I varn you not to lie, Fräulein. Ve know you haff relatives in Chermany.' Ollie, it appeared, was a man of many talents.

'I *do* have relatives in Germany,' Rosalie said, half to the bedroom and half to Carella and Hawes, who were watching her intently. 'The family name used to be Wagner. It got bastardized.'

'Vatch your language, Fräulein!' Ollie called from the other room.

'Do you speak German?' Carella asked, again conversationally.

'Yes.'

'And you have relatives in Bremen, is that it?'

'In Zeven,' Rosalie said. 'Just outside Bremen.' The hand holding the brandy snifter was trembling.

'Well, nothing wrong with visiting relatives,' Carella said, and handed the passport to her. 'Short trip, though, wasn't it?'

Rosalie took the passport. 'I only had a few days,' she said.

'Vacation, was it?'

'Yes.'

'From your job?'

'Yes.'

'Where do you work?'

'Diamondback Development,' she said. 'Part time.'

'What sort of work do you do for them?'

'Secretarial work,' she said.

Carella looked at the trembling hand holding the brandy snifter. The fingernails on that hand were long and pointed, and painted an emerald-green that matched Rosalie's gown and slippers. 'Oscar Hemmings is a partner in that company, isn't he?'

'Yes, he is.'

'Did he get the job for you?'

'He recommended me for it. As I told you, he's a good friend.'

'Do you work directly *under* him?' Ollie shouted from the other room, and laughed obscenely.

'I work for all three partners,' Rosalie said.

'But only part time.'

'Only when they need me to take dictation or do filing. Like that,' she said.

'Sounds okay to me,' Carella said. 'How we doing in there, Ollie?'

Ollie came back into the living room, perspiring. 'I thought you lived here alone,' he said to Rosalie.

'I do,' she said.

'Then what're all those men's clothes doing in the closet and the dresser drawers?'

'Well,' she said, and shrugged.

'Shirts monogrammed O.H.,' Ollie said. 'That'd be for Oscar Hemmings, wouldn't it?'

'I suppose so,' Rosalie said.

'Yes or no?'

'Yes.'

'What's your *real* relationship with Hemmings?' Ollie asked.

'We're engaged.'

'In *what*?' Ollie said, and laughed.

'He's my fiancé.'

'Why didn't you say so in the first place?'

145

'I didn't want to get him in trouble.'

'What kind of trouble were you thinking about?'

'You said something about arson.'

'Well, as you can see,' Ollie said, 'we ain't trying to get him in any trouble at all. Nor you, either.'

'Mmm,' Rosalie said.

'We're sorry to have bothered you,' Carella said. 'We'd like to keep in touch, though, so don't leave the city or anything, okay?'

'I don't plan on leaving the city.'

'What he means is don't go visiting no relatives in Germany,' Ollie said.

'I know what he means. Who's going to pay for having my lock fixed?'

'What lock is that?' Ollie said.

'On the *door*,' Rosalie said. 'What the hell lock do you think?'

'Gee,' Ollie said innocently, 'that was busted when we got here.'

*

It was beginning to look like something – but they didn't know what.

They only knew that the case was getting very hot, and the best way to solve a case that's beginning to sizzle is to stick with it as advised in the Detective Division's mimeographed flyer titled *Investigation of Homicides and Suspicious Deaths*: 'This is *your* case . . . stick with the investigation and *don't do* unimportant jobs.' Whether or not the Detective Division would have considered the examination of a World Atlas an 'important' job was open to question. But a glance at that book revealed immediately that not only was Bremen close to Zeven (where Rosalie Waggener claimed she had relatives), it was *also* close to Bremerhaven – where a man named Erhard Bachmann ran a firm called Bachmann Speditionsfirma.

It may have been coincidental that Rosalie had arrived in Bremen on July 25, and that Bachmann had received payment for packing Grimm's little wooden beasts the very next day, according to his letter of July 26, written to Grimm. It may also have been coincidental that Charlie Harrod's gun had killed Frank Reardon, who had worked for Roger Grimm, who was in turn doing business with a firm in Bremerhaven, some fifty kilometers from Bremen. And the biggest coincidence of all may have been that yet another man associated with Diamondback Development had served time at Castleview State Penitentiary while Roger Grimm himself was incarcerated there. Alfred Allen Chase's *first* year at Castleview had overlapped Roger Grimm's *last* year there. In effect, the men had served concurrent terms for that period of time. All these seemingly related facts may only have been trains passing in the night. But it didn't look that way to the detectives.

None of the three had had much sleep, but they had all eaten hearty breakfasts in the 83rd's squadroom. They were now ready to head out into the city again, in an attempt to unravel some of the knots. They agreed that their telephone drop would be the 87th's squadroom, and then they left the 83rd. Carella was carrying police photos of Charlie Harrod's dead body. Ollie was carrying a Polaroid camera, and police photos of the members of The Ancient Skulls. Hawes wasn't carrying anything.

It was now eight-thirty AM.

Elizabeth Benjamin was awake and being fed intravenously because her jaw was wired and she could not open her mouth. Neither could she nod or shake her head in answer to police questions. So Ollie stuck a pencil in her right hand and propped up a pad for her, and then asked his questions. Willingly but awkwardly, Elizabeth wrote her answers onto the pad.

'These are police photographs,' he said, 'of six members of a street gang called The Ancient Skulls. We took these pictures up in the squadroom last night when we arrested these guys, and we'd like you to look at them now and tell us if any of them were involved in beating you up. This is a young man named Lewis Coombs. Was he one of your attackers?'

yes

'This is a young man named Avery Evans. Was he one of your attackers?'

yes

'This punk . . . this young man is named Felix Collins. Was he in on the attack?'

No

'How about this one? His name is John Morley.'

No

'This one? Jamison Holder?'

yes!!!

'Here's the last one. Timothy Anderson.'

yes

'Okay now, that was very good, Miss Benjamin,' Ollie said, 'and I know you're tired and I don't want to keep you any longer than I have too. There's just one other thing I need, and that's a picture of you. That's for the district attorney,' Ollie said, 'to help in preparing his case against these punks who hurt you so bad. I can take a picture with this Polaroid I got here, but you're all wired up and all, and I'd prefer having a picture that resembles you more like when you were more yourself, if you know what I mean. Would you have such a picture?'

Elizabeth watched him out of puffed and swollen eyes, picked up the pencil again, and wrote on the pad:

wallet. Nurse.

Ollie asked the nurse to fetch Elizabeth's wallet, and when she brought it to him, he gave it to Elizabeth. Both her legs were in casts to the hip, her broken jaw was wired, her broken ribs taped, and there were bandages covering her bruised face and arms. It was only with great effort that she located the snapshot in the plastic gatefold, extracted it, and handed it to Ollie.

In the photo, she was standing in front of a Diamondback tenement wall, smiling into the sunshine. She was wearing a simple yellow frock and low sandals. She looked quite pretty.

'Thank you,' Ollie said, 'I will show this to the DA.'

He had no intention of showing it to the DA.

*

From a telephone booth across the street from the tenement in which Rosalie Waggener's sumptuous pad was located, Cotton Hawes called the number listed in the Isola directory and waited for Rosalie to answer the phone. When her voice came onto the line at last, it was fuzzy with sleep.

'Hello?' she said.

'Rosalie?' he said.

'Mmm.'

'My name's Dick Coopersmith, I'm from Detroit. I was talking to a man in a bar who said I might enjoy meeting you.'

'What man?' Rosalie said.

'Fellow named Dave Carter. Or Carson. I'm not sure which.'

'You've got the wrong number,' Rosalie said, and hung up.

Hawes shrugged, put the receiver back on the hook, and walked out of the booth. He had only been trying to ascertain whether or not Rosalie was still in the apartment, but he'd figured he might as well take a whack at establishing her occupation at the same time. Some you win, some you lose. He took up position in a doorway some fifteen feet from the phone booth, and hoped Rosalie wouldn't sleep too late and that eventually she'd come out of the building and lead him straight to Oscar Hemmings.

*

In his own squadroom, at his own desk, Steve Carella put in a long-distance call to the prison at Castleview-on-Rawley, and asked to talk to someone in Records. The man who came onto the line identified himself as Peter Yarborough.

'What can I do for you?' he asked.

'This is Detective Steve Carella, the 87th Squad, down here in Isola. I'm looking for a record of correspondence to and from a man who . . .'

'Who'd you say this was?'

'Detective Steve Carella, 87th Squad.'

'Put it in writing, Carella,' Yarborough said. 'We can't answer telephone requests.'

'This is urgent,' Carella said. 'We're investigating homicide and arson.'

'What'd you say your name was?'

'Carella. Steve Carella.'

'Where you calling from, Carella?'

'The squadroom.'

'What's the number there?'

'Frederick 7–8024.'

'I'll get back to you,' Yarborough said, and hung up.

Carella looked at the mouthpiece and then slammed the receiver down onto the cradle. The phone rang twenty minutes later. He lifted the receiver. '87th Squad, Carella,' he said.

'This is Yarborough.'

'Hello, Yarborough,' Carella said.

'I wanted to call you back because how did I know you were *really* a detective?' Yarborough said.

'That's right, you did the right thing,' Carella said.

'I did *better* than the right thing. I first called Headquarters down there in the city and made sure this number was really the number of a detective squadroom.'

'You did very well,' Carella said. 'Can you help with that record of correspondence?'

'I'll try,' Yarborough said. 'What was the prisoner's name?'

'Alfred Allen Chase.'

'When was he here?'

'Started serving his sentence five years ago. Served three and a half.'

'What were you interested in, Carella?'

'I want to know if there was any correspondence between him and a man named Roger Grimm, who's also one of your graduates.'

'Yeah, we get 'em all here, sooner or later,' Yarborough said dryly. 'Any special time period? Some of these lists are a mile long, take me all morning to go through 'em.'

'Grimm was paroled in June, four years ago. Can you start there?'

'Yeah, I guess so,' Yarborough said reluctantly. 'Let me get back to you.'

*

At ten minutes to ten Fat Ollie Weeks walked into the second-floor offices of Diamondback Development. There were two men seated at the long table in front of the wall of photographs. One of them was Robinson Worthy. The other was a black man Ollie had never seen before.

'Good morning,' Ollie said cheerily. 'Just happened to be in the neighborhood and thought I'd stop by.'

'Good morning,' Worthy said. His voice was frosty, his eyes wary.

'I don't believe I've had the pleasure,' Ollie said to the other man.

'This is my other partner,' Worthy said. 'Oscar Hemmings.'

'Pleased to meet you, Mr Hemmings,' Ollie said, and extended his hand.

Hemmings was a handsome man of perhaps fifty, impeccably dressed in a brown lightweight business suit, beige shirt with a button-down collar, simple tie of a deeper shade of brown. His face was craggy, a strong sledge-hammer nose, well-pronounced cheekbones, a firm mouth, a square jaw. His hair was turning gray, styled to hide the fact that it was thinning a bit. His handshake was firm. He smiled thinly and said in a very low voice, 'Nice to meet you, Detective Weeks.'

Ollie did not miss the fact that Hemmings knew who he was. This meant that Worthy and Chase had discussed him with their partner. He filed away the information, and said, 'I really didn't just *happen* to be in the neighborhood. I came up here deliberately.' Worthy and Hemmings said nothing. 'First of all, I wanted to apologize,' Ollie said. 'I really behaved like an asshole yesterday, Mr Worthy. I don't know what got into me.' The Diamondback partners still said nothing. 'Also, I wanted

151

to tell you we got the people we think killed Charlie Harrod. Least of all, we *know* they beat up Harrod's girl friend. I just came from the hospital, where I got positive identification on four of them, so I thought you'd be happy to hear that.'

'Yes, we're very happy to hear that,' Worthy said.

'You fellows put in a long week, don't you?' Ollie said. 'Work Saturdays and all, huh?'

'So do you, it seems,' Hemmings said, and again smiled his razor-blade smile.

'No, no, I'm off today,' Ollie said. 'Think I'll take in a ball game or something.' He paused, and then said, 'By the way, Mr Hemmings, we stopped by at an apartment we thought was yours because we were trying to locate you this morning . . .'

'Oh?' Hemmings said.

'Yeah, when we picked up these guys, you know, who we think killed Harrod.'

'Yes?' Hemmings said.

'Yes,' Ollie said. 'Yes. We wanted somebody in the company to know about it, and I was a little embarrassed about contacting Mr Worthy here because of the way I hassled him yesterday.' He smiled in apology. 'So we went over to the apartment on St Sebastian.'

'Why didn't you simply telephone?' Hemmings asked.

'Well, it was close by, no sweat.' Ollie paused. 'We met the girl living there.'

'Yes?' Hemmings said.

'Yes. Girl named Rosalie Waggener. Nice girl.'

Hemmings said nothing.

'She ought to get the door fixed,' Ollie said. 'The lock's busted.' He smiled again. 'Well, just thought I'd let you know everything's all wrapped up, and I'm sorry I gave you such a hard time. I'll see you, huh? Keep up the good work here in Diamondback.' He chopped his beefy hand into the air in farewell, and went out. In the hallway outside, he put his ear to the frosted-glass door and listened. Someone was dialing a telephone. He expected that would be Oscar Hemmings trying to reach his little white bimbo. Ollie smiled and went downstairs and out of the building.

The streets were already beginning to blister under the on-slaught of the early-morning sun. Ollie walked two blocks up Landis, turned left, and continued walking north toward the River Harb. A green panel truck was parked in front of an abandoned warehouse facing the river. The man at the wheel of the truck was dozing, a cap pulled down over his eyes, a matchstick between his teeth. Ollie rapped on the partially closed window, and the man jerked suddenly awake.

'I'm Weeks,' Ollie said. 'You the guy from the Motor Pool?'

'Yeah,' the man said. 'Halloran.'

Ollie stepped back and looked over the truck. 'They sent a good one for a change,' he said. 'It must be a miracle. Most of these goddamn trucks, everybody in the neighborhood knows it's taking pictures. This is a nice one, company name painted on the side and everything. Even a phony telephone number. Real classy.'

'The number's hooked into a phone at Headquarters down-town,' Halloran said. 'Anybody calls it to check whether this is a phony truck, a guy answers and gives the name of the company painted on the side there.'

'Ah yes,' Ollie said in his W. C. Fields voice, 'very classy, very classy indeed.' In his natural voice he said. 'I got to make a phone call, Halloran. Soon as I'm done, we're heading for 2914 Landis. Okay?'

'Sure, why not?' Halloran said, and shrugged.

*

When the telephone rang on Carella's desk, he thought it might be Yarborough calling back from Castleview. Instead, it was Ollie Weeks.

'Carella,' he said, 'this is Ollie. Has Hawes called in yet?'

'No. Why?'

'I found Oscar Hemmings, there's no need for him to stick with the girl.'

'I'll tell him if he calls.'

'There's one other thing,' Ollie said. 'He was up there alone with Worthy, which means I can't get nothing on Chase. You want to handle that from your end?

'You thinking of the IS?'

'Yeah, Chase has a record, so they're sure to have mug shots of him.'

'Will do,' Carella said.

'I got to get moving,' Ollie said. 'Before my jigaboo friends decide to leave without me.'

*

Rosalie Waggener came down the front steps of 1137 St Sebastian at a little past ten-thirty. She was wearing bell-bottomed, hip-hugger tan pants, a scoop-necked, horizontally striped top, and brown low-heeled shoes. In her right hand, she was clutching a small brown pocketbook, which she waved frantically at a passing taxicab the moment she stepped onto the curb.

Cotton Hawes, watching from the doorway across the street, did not know that a call to the squadroom would have advised him to drop the tail. He knew only that he had better get to his car damn fast, because the cab had already squealed to a stop just ahead and was now backing up to the curb to pick up Rosalie. Hawes's car was parked halfway up the block. He began walking swiftly, turning once to see Rosalie getting into the taxi. He had just climbed behind the wheel, and was starting the car, when the taxi flashed by.

With a little luck, Hawes figured he would catch up at the next traffic light.

*

In the rear of the panel truck, sitting behind a camera equipped with a telescopic lens and mounted on a tripod, Ollie Weeks sat behind the equivalent of a one-way-two-way mirror, waiting to take photographs of Worthy and Hemmings the moment they came out of the building across the street. Ollie was looking through a clear pane of glass. The other side of the glass was painted green, like the side of the truck, and then lettered over in yellow paint with the name of the fake company, its address, and the telephone number of the phone downtown at Headquarters.

There was a steady stream of traffic, mostly women, into 2914 Landis. Ollie figured they were heading up to BLACK FASHIONS on the third floor. Ollie watched the women through the telescopic lens. One thing you had to say for black broads, they had good legs.

Hemmings and Worthy did not come out of the building until twenty minutes past eleven. The moment they appeared at the top of the steps, coming through the door, Ollie began taking pictures. He cocked the camera and pressed the shutter release a total of thirteen times before they reached the sidewalk, and then he got three more shots of them moving away in profile. Ollie nodded in satisfaction and rapped on the panel leading to the front of the truck.

Halloran slid it open. 'Yeah?'

'I need to go downtown to the IS,' Ollie said.

'You finished here?' Halloran asked.

'Yeah. But I got to get this stuff developed and printed.'

'I'm supposed to take the truck back when you're finished.'

'You can take me downtown first.'

'This ain't a goddamn taxi,' Halloran said, but he started the truck and pointed it downtown.

*

'Carella?'

'Yes?'

'This is Yarborough. I got that information you want.'

'Go ahead,' Carella said.

'This Roger Grimm character was paroled four years ago. Chase was still here at the time, had already served a year and a little more of his sentence.'

'Right, I've got that already.'

'Okay. The minute Grimm got out, he began writing to Chase. Correspondence was hot and heavy for about six months. Chase wrote to Grimm, and vice versa, at least once a week, sometimes twice. Then all at once, the correspondence stopped. You know what I think? These guys maybe had a thing here in prison, you know what I mean? Lovers, you know? You'd be surprised what goes on up here.'

'Yes, I'd be surprised,' Carella said.

'I'm only speculating,' Yarborough said. 'Maybe they were just friends, who knows? You know the one about the lady with the monkeys?'

'No, which one is that?' Carella said.

'This lady comes into a taxidermist with two dead monkeys, you know, and she says she wants them stuffed. So the taxidermist says, "Yes, lady, I'll stuff the monkeys. You want them mounted, too?" And the lady thinks for a minute and says, "No, they were only friends. Just have them shaking hands."' Yarborough burst out laughing. Carella, who had remembered the joke after the first line, chuckled politely. 'So maybe Grimm and Chase were only friends, who knows?' Yarborough said, still laughing. 'Anyway, they wrote to each other a lot after Grimm got out.'

'You wouldn't know whether or not they were cellmates, would you?'

'That's another department,' Yarborough said.

'When did the correspondence between them stop?'

'Six months after Grimm got paroled.'

'Okay,' Carella said. 'Thanks a lot.'

'*Wait* a minute,' Yarborough said. 'Two other things.'

'I'm sorry, I thought you were . . .'

'They began writing to each other again just before *Chase* got paroled. Chase wrote the first letter, and then Grimm answered, and then they exchanged maybe a dozen more letters before Chase finally left this joint. That's the first thing.'

'What's the second thing?'

'The second thing is I need a letter from you formally requesting this information.'

'You already *gave* me the information,' Carella said. 'Why do you need a letter from me *requesting* it?'

'To cover me. Just in case.'

'In case of what?'

'I don't *know* what. Just in case. Send me the letter, Carella.'

'Okay,' Carella said, and sighed. 'Thanks again.'

'How's it down there in the city?' Yarborough asked.

'Hot,' Carella said.

'Yeah, here too,' Yarborough said, and hung up.

Carella pressed one of the buttons in the receiver rest, held it down for a second, and then released it, getting a dial tone. He called the Identification Section and told the man he spoke to that he urgently needed some eight-by-ten glossies of Alfred Allen Chase's mug shots.

The man listened to the request, and then said, 'This is Saturday, pal.'

'Yeah, it's Saturday here, too,' Carella said.

'I don't even know if there's anybody next door in the Photo Unit.'

'*Find* somebody,' Carella said.

*

Downtown on High Street, the man in the Photographic Unit took the roll of film from Ollie's hand and said, 'You're gonna have to wait. I just got a rush order from next door.'

'Yeah, well make it snappy, willya?' Ollie said. '*This* is a rush order, too.' He went down the hall to the phone booths, dialed the 87th, and when he got Carella, said, 'I took more'n a dozen pictures, we're bound to get one or two good ones. You heard from Hawes yet?'

'No, not yet.'

'What the hell's the matter with him? Don't he know he's supposed to check in?'

'I guess he's busy,' Carella said.

'What'd you find out at Castleview?'

'Chase and Grimm knew each other. They corresponded regularly.'

'Just what we figured,' Ollie said. 'Did you get those pictures from the IS?'

'Should be here in a little while, I hope.'

'Okay, I'll see you soon,' Ollie said.

He had not told Carella where he was, and Carella did not think to ask. Nor did the man in the Photographic Unit tell Ollie that the rush order from next door was earmarked for a detective named Steve Carella of the 87th Squad. He did not tell Ollie because it was none of Ollie's business. Ollie didn't ask him anything about the rush order because all Ollie wanted was his own damn pictures and fast. Besides, Carella had already assured him the mug shots of Chase should be up at the squadroom in just a little while. Ollie left High Street with his own eight-by-ten glossies at a quarter to one. The package to Carella from the PU (as it was affectionately called by any detective who'd ever had to wait for photographs) did not arrive at the squadroom until almost one-thirty. They had still not heard from Hawes, so they decided to hit Reardon's landlady all by their lonesomes.

*

Rosalie Waggener's taxi had traveled directly up Ainsley Avenue until it reached the Hamilton Bridge. Actually there were *two* Hamilton Bridges in the city, one of them on the northern side of Isola, crossing the River Harb into the next state, and formally called the *Alexander* Hamilton Bridge. This was not to be confused with the plain old *Hamilton* Bridge, which crossed the Diamondback River up around Piney Hill Terrace (upon which there was not a single pine tree) and connected Isola and Riverhead, which were both parts of the same state and, in fact, the same city. If you asked anyone in the city for directions to the Hamilton Bridge, they would invariably give you directions to the Alexander Hamilton Bridge. In fact, odds were nine-to-five that nobody in the city even *knew* there was a bridge simply called the Hamilton, less than a block long and spanning the Diamondback River, which incidentally became the River Dix a little further west – it was all very complicated, though not as complicated as the city of Bologna, Italy.

The cab continued south into Riverhead, crossing the old College Road and then turning and proceeding west on Marlowe Avenue for several blocks. It finally pulled up before a red-brick apartment building on Marlowe, a few blocks from the elevated train tracks on Geraldson Avenue. Hawes pulled his own car into the curb, cut the ignition, and watched as Rosalie, some seven car lengths ahead, got out of the taxi and went directly into the building. He waited a respectable five minutes, figuring a building so tall *had* to be an elevator building, and not wanting her to be waiting in the lobby when he went inside. At the end of that time, he went in, found the mailboxes, and began checking out the nameplates.

There were ten stories in the building, with six apartments

on each floor. According to the nameplates, Oscar Hemmings did not live in the building.

But on the mailbox for Apartment 45, there was a plate engraved with a name Hawes recognized.

He squinted at the name, and then scratched his head.

*

'My husband is downtown buying hardware,' Barbara Loomis said. 'Anything I can do for you?'

She was wearing very tight, very short navy-blue shorts and a pink shirt with the tails knotted just under her breasts. 'Come in,' she said, 'come in. Nobody going to bite you.'

They went into the apartment and sat at the kitchen table. Fat Ollie kept trying to look into her blouse. He was sure she wasn't wearing a bra, and the top three buttons of the blouse were unbuttoned. Carella spread the photographs on the tabletop – the mug shots of Alfred Allen Chase; the police photographer's shots of Charlie Harrod in death, eyes wide and staring up at the camera; the snapshot of Elizabeth Benjamin standing against the tenement wall, smiling; and the front and side shots Ollie had taken of Robinson Worthy and Oscar Hemmings that morning.

'Recognize any of these people?' he asked Barbara.

'Yeah, sure I do,' Barbara said. 'What happened to the big red-headed cop? How come he didn't come back with these?'

'Won't we do?' Ollie said, and grinned.

'Which of them do you recognize?' Carella asked.

'You fellows want a beer?' Barbara said.

'No, thanks,' Carella said.

'I wouldn't mind one,' Ollie said, and watched Barbara's behind when she rose and walked to the refrigerator. He winked at Carella and grinned again.

Barbara came back to the table, set the beer before Ollie, and then looked down at the pictures. 'This is the girl Frank shacked up with those two nights,' she said, and pointed to the picture of Elizabeth Benjamin.

'And the others?' Carella said.

'Two of those men came to see Frank at the end of July.'

159

'Which ones?' Carella asked.

'This one and this one,' Barbara said, her forefinger tapping first Charlie Harrod's head and then Robinson Worthy's.

'Recognize the other man in that picture?' Carella asked.

'This one?' she asked. She lifted the picture Ollie had taken, and peered at Oscar Hemmings. 'No,' she said. 'Never saw him here. That doesn't mean he's never been here, it just means I never saw him.'

'Okay. How about this man?' Carella asked, and shoved the picture of Alfred Allen Chase across the table.

'Nope, never saw him either,' Barbara said, and turned to Ollie and smiled. 'How's the beer?' she asked.

'Delicious,' Ollie said. 'Just delicious, m'little chickadee,' and Barbara giggled girlishly.

In the car riding uptown to the squadroom, Carella said, 'Worthy and Harrod. They're definitely the ones who made contact with Reardon, which means Diamondback Development burned out Grimm.'

'Right,' Ollie said. 'I think that lady can be banged, you know that?'

'I don't get it,' Carella said.

'You know what she said to me?'

'What?' Carella asked absently.

'She said her bedroom is air-conditioned. I tell you that lady can be banged, Carella.'

'It was Rosalie Waggener who went to Bremen, right?' Carella said. 'And she's Hemmings' girl friend, right?'

'Right,' Ollie said. 'Yep, I think that lady can very definitely be banged.'

'Rosalie flew to Bremen on the day before Grimm's packer acknowledged receipt of payment. Grimm's check *couldn't* have got there by then, so somebody must've made payment in person. And that had to be Rosalie.'

'I think I'll give that lady a call tonight.'

'But what's the connection, Ollie? Why the hell would Hemmings' girl be paying Grimm's bills while Hemmings' company is planning to burn down Grimm's warehouse? It doesn't make sense. It doesn't make sense at all.'

It made even less sense when they got back to the squad-room. Hawes was waiting for them there, and he reported that Rosalie Waggener had spent almost an hour in an apartment on Marlowe Avenue before heading back to Isola again.

The mailbox in the Marlowe Avenue lobby had carried a plate with the name Alfred Allen Chase engraved on it.

10

They picked up Rosalie Waggener at four o'clock that afternoon and took her to the squadroom. They told her they were not charging her with anything, but that they had reasonable grounds to believe she had information pertinent to their investigation, and would appreciate her answering a few questions. Rosalie said she would answer any questions they wanted to ask, but not without a lawyer present. They explained again that she was not being charged with anything, and when she insisted on a lawyer, they explained that they could force her to testify before a grand jury, but they did not want to go to all that trouble since she was not being charged with anything.

Reluctantly, Rosalie agreed to answer their questions.

'According to your passport,' Carella said, 'you entered West Germany through the Bremen airport on July twenty-fifth, is that correct?'

'Yes, that's correct,' Rosalie said.

'And you returned to the United States on July twenty-seventh, is that also correct?'

'Yes,' Rosalie said.

'You told us you were visiting your relatives in Zeven.'

'That's right.'

'We want to know the names, addresses, and telephone numbers of your relatives in Zeven,' Carella said.

'Why?'

'Because we're going to check with the German police to make sure they exist.'

'They exist,' Rosalie said.

'Then give us their names.'

'I don't have to.'

'That's right, you don't have to. Not here, you don't. Before a grand jury, you do. It's up to you.'

'Will the police call them? The German police?'

'Yes, that's what we'll request.'

'Why?'

'To make sure you were with them.'

'I was.'

'Then what are their names?'

'They're very old people. I don't want them bothered by the police. Anyway, what's this got to do with your investigation? You said I had information that might . . .'

'That's right.'

'What information?'

'Do you know a man named Roger Grimm?'

'No.'

'Did you visit Bremerhaven while you were in West Germany?'

'No.'

'Are you familiar with a firm called Bachmann Speditions-firma in Bremerhaven?'

'No.'

'Why'd you go see Alfred Chase this afternoon?'

'Who said I . . . ?'

'I followed you there,' Hawes said. '5361 Marlowe Avenue. Chase is in Apartment 45.'

'Did you go there or not?' Ollie asked.

'I went there.'

'Why?'

'Mr Chase had some correspondence he wanted to answer. I told you, I do part-time secretarial work for . . .'

'Why didn't you answer it at the office?'

'The office is closed on Saturdays.'

'I was there this morning,' Ollie said. 'It was open.'

'Well, I guess Mr Chase didn't feel like going in today. I'm not the boss, you know. If they ask me to go up to Riverhead, I go.' Rosalie shrugged. 'I'm not the boss.'

'Who *is* the boss?'

'They're three partners.'

'I thought Hemmings was your boy friend.'

'He is. But I work for the company. That has nothing to do with it. Oscar has nothing to do with it. I mean, if one of the

163

bosses asks me to do something, I have to do it. It's a job. If *your* boss asks you to do something, *you* do it, don't you?'

'I'm not engaged to my boss,' Ollie said dryly.

'All I'm trying to say is it's a job like any other job. I do what they ask me to do.'

'What do they ask you to do? Besides taking dictation and typing letters?'

'Secretarial work. All kinds of secretarial work.'

'Did they ask you to go to Germany?'

'No, I went there to visit my relatives.'

'What are their names?' Carella asked again.

'I'll give you their names if you promise not to bother them.'

'I can't promise that. I intend to place a transatlantic call the minute you give me the information.'

'Why? What the hell's so important about my relatives?'

'We're trying to find out why you went to Germany, Miss Waggener.'

'Did Diamondback Development send you there?'

'No.'

'Did Roger Grimm?'

'I never heard of Roger Grimm.'

'Did you take money to Germany?'

'Money? What do you mean? Of course, I took money.'

'How much?'

'Enough for expenses. In traveler's checks.'

'How much?'

'I forget. A little more than a thousand, I think.'

'Did you spend it all?'

'No, not all of it.'

'Then you've still got traveler's checks you didn't cash, is that right?'

'Well . . . yes, I suppose so. Maybe I did spend all of it.'

'Did you or didn't you?'

'Yes, I spent all of it.'

'A minute ago you said you *didn't* spend all of it.'

'I was mistaken.'

'Then you *don't* have any uncashed traveler's checks.'

'That's right, I don't.'

'Where'd you buy the traveler's checks?'

'At a bank.'

'Which bank?'

'I forget. One of the banks downtown.'

'When did you buy them?'

'A few days before I left.'

'That would be . . .' Carella picked up the desk calendar and studied it. 'You left on July twenty-fifth, which was a Thursday, so you bought the checks sometime before then, right?'

'Yes.'

'Sometime that week?'

'Yes.'

'That would have been either Monday, Tuesday, or Wednesday, right? July twenty-second, -third, or -fourth. Is that when you bought them, Miss Waggener?'

'Yes.'

'What *kind* of traveler's checks?'

'American Express.'

'You won't mind if we call American Express, will you?'

'Why do you want to call them?'

'To find out about the checks.'

'It was only a thousand dollars or so, what's so important about that? Everybody uses traveler's checks. I don't see what's so . . .'

'Some people use cash,' Hawes said.

'Yes, I suppose so,' Rosalie said.

'Did you take any cash with you?' Carella asked. 'In addition to the traveler's checks?'

'A little, I guess. I really don't remember.'

'How much?' Ollie asked.

'Just a little. A hundred dollars or so.'

'And that's all you took to Germany, right? A thousand dollars in traveler's checks . . .'

'Well, a thousand more or less. I don't remember the exact amount.'

'Well, let's say a thousand, okay? A thousand in traveler's checks and about a hundred in cash.'

'Yes, that's right.'

'Okay, let's call American Express,' Ollie said.

'They probably won't have a record,' Rosalie said quickly.

'Why not?'

'Because . . . I don't remember whether they were American Express checks or some other kind.'

'What other kind do you think they might have been?'

'I don't remember. I just asked for traveler's checks. I can't really remember which kind they gave me.'

'There aren't too many companies issuing traveler's checks in this city,' Carella said. 'If you don't mind, we'll call them all.'

'I . . .'

'Yes?' Carella said.

'Actually, I took cash,' she said.

'Then why'd you lie about it?'

'Because I wasn't sure how much cash you're allowed to take out of the country. I thought it might be illegal or something. I'm not familiar with the law.'

'How much money *did* you take out?'

'I told you. A little more than a thousand.'

'In cash.'

'Yes.'

'You're *sure* it was in cash. A minute ago you said it was in traveler's checks, but now you're saying it was cash. Are you sure about that?'

'Oh yes, I'm sure.'

'And you're also sure about the amount.'

'The amount?'

'Yes. A thousand dollars, is that right?'

'More or less.'

'Which?'

'What?'

'Which was it? Was it more than a thousand, or less than a thousand?'

'More.'

'How much more?'

'Oh, twelve hundred, thirteen hundred, something like that.'

'Where'd you get the money?'

'I had it. I saved it.'

'Where'd you save it?'

'I kept it in the apartment.'

'You didn't keep it in a bank?'

'No.'

'You figured it was safe to leave thirteen hundred dollars in an apartment in Diamondback?' Ollie asked incredulously.

'Yes. I've never been robbed. I've been living there for almost three months, and I've never been robbed. I figured it was safe.'

'Where'd you live before then?'

'Downtown. In the Quarter.'

'Where'd you meet Oscar Hemmings?'

'At a party, I think.'

'When?'

'Oh, six, seven months ago.'

'How long have you been engaged?'

'Oh, four or five months.'

'You got engaged before you moved into the apartment on St Sebastian?'

'Yes.'

'Who paid to have the apartment redone?'

'Oscar.'

'Oscar personally? Or Diamondback Development?'

'Diamondback Development, I think. That's their business, you know. Buying these old buildings and fixing them up.'

'Oh, have *all* the apartments in that building been fixed up?'

'Yes, I think so.'

'But not the outside of the building.'

'No, not the outside.'

'Why's that?'

'Gee, I don't know,' Rosalie said. 'Maybe they didn't want to spend the extra money. To fix up the outside, I mean.'

'Who else lives in that building?' Hawes asked.

'Lots of people.'

'Know any of them?'

'I don't have much to do with my neighbors,' Rosalie said.

'You say you met Oscar six or seven months ago. Where

was that? In Diamondback, or down in the Quarter?'

'Well, actually, I met him in Vegas.'

'Vegas? What were you doing there?'

'I used to go there weekends. When I was living on the Coast.'

'Oh, did you live in California?' Hawes asked.

'Yes. I was born in California. I only came here recently. After I met Oscar.'

'What kind of work did you do on the Coast?' Ollie asked.

'Secretarial.'

'Full or part time?'

'Well, part time mostly.'

'Who'd you work for?'

'Lots of different companies.'

'And you used to go to Las Vegas every weekend, is that right?'

'Well, not *every* weekend.'

'Just *some* weekends.'

'Yes, just some.'

'And that's where you met Oscar Hemmings.'

'Yes.'

'At a party there, right?'

'Yes, at a party.'

'And then you came East and started working for Diamondback Development.'

'Yes.'

'And living with Oscar.'

'Yes. After we got engaged.'

'In a building renovated by Diamondback Development.'

'Yes.'

'Are you a hooker, Miss Waggener?' Hawes asked.

'No. Oh, no.'

'Ever been arrested, Miss Waggener?'

'No.'

'Sure about that?'

'Well, minor things.'

'Like what?'

'Traffic violations.'

'Here or in California?'

'California.'

'Where'd you live out there?'

'In LA.'

'Would you mind if we called the Los Angeles Police Department to find out whether or not you were ever arrested for anything more serious than a traffic violation?'

'I don't see any reason for you to do that.'

'Why not?'

'I may decide to go back to California one day. I don't want the police there to have me listed as somebody questionable.'

'Questionable?'

'Well, somebody you were asking questions about.'

'You don't want us to call the German police, you don't want us to call the LA police, you don't want us to call American Express, or any of the other traveler's checks companies . . .'

'I took cash with me, I told you that.'

'That's a lot of people you don't want us to call, Miss Waggener.'

'You said I'm not being charged with anything. Okay, so why should I allow you to pry into my personal life?'

'We're going to call Los Angeles, anyway. We're also going to call Las Vegas.'

'Why?'

'To see if you've got an arrest record.'

'Okay, okay,' Rosalie said.

'We can call?'

'No, you don't have to call.'

'You want to tell us about it?'

'I was arrested once for prostitution on the Coast.'

'Uh-huh,' Hawes said.

'You still hooking?' Ollie asked.

'No.'

'What's that fancy building on St Sebastian? It's a whore-house, ain't it?'

'Gee, I couldn't tell you. It's where I live.'

'Is Oscar Hemmings a pimp?'

'No. Oh, no,' Rosalie said.

'We're going to visit that building again, you know,' Carella said. 'To find out who else is living there.'

'Well, they're just ordinary tenants,' Rosalie said.

'Like *you*?' Ollie asked.

'I haven't had any trouble with the police since that time in LA,' Rosalie said.

'That only means you haven't been *caught* lately,' Ollie said.

'Well,' Rosalie said, and shrugged. 'Is it okay if I smoke?'

'Sure,' Ollie said, and then held a lighted match to the cigarette she took from her handbag.

'What do you know about Diamondback Development?' Carella asked.

'Oh, not much.'

'Who put up the money to form the company, would you know that?'

'No, I'm sorry. I wouldn't know that.'

'Was it Oscar Hemmings?'

'I really couldn't say.'

'You want to tell us why you *really* went to visit Chase?'

'I already told you. To do some letters for him.'

'Let's drop the secretarial crap, okay?' Ollie said.

'That's what I am,' Rosalie said flatly. 'A secretary. I've got no record in this city, and you can't prove I'm anything *but* a secretary.'

'Unless we catch you screwing a sailor,' Ollie said.

'I don't screw sailors,' Rosalie said. 'Not even on the Coast, I didn't screw sailors.'

'What *do* you screw?' Ollie asked. 'Niggers?'

'Will you please cut that out?' Carella said.

'Cut what out?' Ollie asked.

'Anyway, my private life is none of your business,' Rosalie said.

'Unless you do it for money.'

'Everybody does everything for money,' Rosalie answered.

'Who gave you the money you took to Germany?' Carella asked.

'I told you. I saved it.'

'Are you going to tell us the names of your relatives?'

'No.'

'Then we're going to have to get a subpoena requiring you to testify before the grand jury. Let me explain this fully to you, Miss Waggener. We're investigating an arson, and we have good cause to believe that Diamondback Development was somehow involved with it. We have enough evidence right this minute to arrest Robinson Worthy . . .'

'Then arrest him,' Rosalie said.

'. . . and charge him with complicity in the crime of arson, in which case the grand jury would subpoena you to testify as a witness.'

'A witness to *what*? Arson? You're out of your mind.'

'If you tell us what you know, you can save yourself a lot of trouble later. What do you say?'

'I've told you everything I know.'

'Let *me* tell you what the grand jury's going to ask, okay?'

'Sure.'

'They're going to inform you, first of all, that the man whose factory was burned down is named Roger Grimm. They're also going to inform you that he was doing business with a packing firm called Bachmann Speditionsfirma in Bremerhaven, and that Bachmann acknowledged receiving payment for his services on July twenty-sixth, a day after you arrived in Bremen, which is about fifty kilometers from Bremerhaven. They are then going to ask you, under oath, whether or not you delivered any amount of cash to Bachmann on the date mentioned in his letter. If you refuse to answer . . .'

'Why would I refuse? I never heard of Erhard Bachmann, and I never delivered any money to him.'

'Then how do you know his full name?' Carella said instantly.

'What?' Rosalie said.

'How do you know it's *Erhard* Bachmann?'

'Erhard's a common German name,' Rosalie said.

'So's Fritz,' Ollie said.

'I . . . I don't know how I happened to . . . to guess it.'

'Maybe she's in this deeper than we figured,' Ollie said, in an apparent confidential aside to Carella.

'Maybe so,' Carella said. 'You think we can charge both Worthy *and* her?'

'I don't see why not,' Hawes said.

'Charge me with what?' Rosalie said.

'Arson. Accessory to the crime of arson.'

'I didn't have anything to do with burning down Grimm's warehouse,' Rosalie said. 'All I did . . .'

'Yeah, *what*?' Ollie said.

'I took the money to Germany.'

'What money?'

'The money Alfie gave me.'

'Who's Alfie? Are you talking about Chase?'

'Yes.'

'You took money from Chase and delivered it to Bachmann?'

'Yes.'

'Cash?'

'Yes.'

'How much?'

Rosalie hesitated.

'How *much*, goddamnit!' Ollie shouted.

'Half a million dollars,' Rosalie said.

'For what? What was Chase buying?'

'I don't know. I only had instructions to deliver the money.'

'Whose money was it? Chase's or Diamondback Development's?'

'I don't know.'

'Let's put it another way, Miss Waggener. Did Oscar Hemmings or Robinson Worthy know about your trip to Germany?'

'No.'

'They did *not* know you went to Germany with five hundred thousand dollars that Chase gave you?'

'That's right.'

'I thought you were living with Hemmings.'

'I am. I told him I was going to the Coast, to visit my mother.'

'Why'd you lie to him?'

'Because he . . . he can get mean sometimes. He . . . beats me sometimes.'

'What's with you and Chase?' Ollie asked.

'Nothing.'

'Nothing? And he handed you five hundred grand to take to Germany for him? Come off it, sweetie!'

'All right, we . . . we have a thing.'

'Does Hemmings know about this "thing"?'

'Of course not.'

'You're fooling around with Chase behind Hemmings' back, is that right?'

'We're not fooling around, we're in love.'

'Oh, for*give* me,' Ollie said, bowing from the waist. 'I didn't realize it was *love*. Please *do* forgive me.'

'Why didn't you tell Hemmings you were going to Germany?' Carella asked.

'Alfie asked me not to.'

'Was it Alfie's own money you took to Germany?'

'I don't know.'

'Well, if Alfie asked you *not* to tell his partners about the trip to Germany . . .'

'That's right.'

'Then it *must* have been his own money, wouldn't you say? Unless he stole it from the company.'

'Alfie is not a thief!'

'Then it was his own money, right?'

'I guess so.'

'Yes or no?'

'Yes.'

'He told you it was his own money?'

'Yes, he told me.'

'Where'd he get that kind of money?'

'I don't know.'

'Why'd he give it to Erhard Bachmann?'

'I don't know.'

'You don't know anything about the deal with Bachmann?'

'Nothing.'

'Has it got something to do with little wooden animals?'

'I don't know.'

'Why'd you double-cross Hemmings?' Hawes asked.

'I *didn't*!' Rosalie said indignantly. 'Alfie offered me something better, that's all.'

'Better than marriage?'

'Marriage? What are you talking about?'

'You said you and Hemmings were engaged.'

'No,' Rosalie said. 'I work for him, pure and simple. I'm a whore, okay? I'm part of a stable, okay? And I'm sick of it. Which is why I threw in with Alfie.'

'How many girls in the stable?' Ollie asked.

'About thirty.'

'All in that building on St Sebastian?'

'No. There's only twelve of us there. Oscar's got two other places, I don't know exactly where.'

'Who's on the take?' Ollie asked.

'I don't know what you mean.'

'Who's the cop being paid off? You can't have a steady stream of johns marching into a building without somebody noticing. Now, who's being paid off?'

'It's not a steady stream,' Rosalie said. 'It's a very high-priced operation.'

'How much do you get?'

'Two, three hundred a night.'

'And you say Alfie offered you a better deal?'

'Not *that* kind of deal. Not prostitution. He promised he'd talk to Oscar and get me out of the life. He said if I stuck with him there'd be lots of money for both of us in the future.'

'Money?' Ollie said. 'My, my. And here I thought it was only love.'

'Money, too,' Rosalie said.

'How much money?'

'Alfie said there'd be millions. He said he'd be a millionaire.'

'Where'd Alfie get the five hundred grand he sent to Germany?' Ollie asked.

'I don't know.'

'Is he in on the whorehouse operation?'

'No. That's Oscar's alone.'

'Is Oscar the moneyman behind Diamondback Development?'

'I think so. I don't know. I really don't know too much about the company's finances.'

'Are they buying those buildings to convert into whorehouses?'

'I really don't know.'

'But you said they're not into that end of it. That's Oscar's alone.'

'That's right.'

'So what *are* they into?'

'I don't know.'

'What's Alfie's business with Erhard Bachmann?'

'I don't know.'

'Was Bachmann expecting you when you got to Germany?'

'Yes. But I used a phony name. Alfie told me to use a phony name.'

'What did Bachmann say when you gave him the money?'

'He said "*Danke sehr*."'

That was the end of their little chat with Rosalie Waggener. They figured, by that time, that she had either told them all she knew or all she was willing to tell. They thanked her very much (in English), and asked her to wait in the room down the hall. From what they could gather, Chase and Grimm seemed to be equal partners in the little-wooden-animal business. Without Worthy and Hemmings knowing about it, Chase had paid $500,000 of his own money to Grimm's packer in Germany, and Grimm (before his devastating warehouse fire) had been ready to pay *another* $500,000 for the cargo when it reached America. According to Grimm's own estimate, the resale value of the cargo was one million dollars. The three cops investigating the case knew very little about high-level business transactions involving astronomical figures. They knew only that tangled are the webs we weave when first we practice to deceive, and they further knew that nobody invests a million bucks hoping merely to break even.

It looked like time for a little game of poker.

11

Ollie found Oscar Hemmings in the apartment he shared with Rosalie, supervising the repair of the broken door lock. The locksmith got very nervous when he saw the gun in Ollie's hand. He dropped his screwdriver, and then immediately began packing his tools. Hemmings, in his shirt sleeves, the collar of the shirt open, the sleeves rolled up, the monogram O.H. over the breast pocket, very calmly asked Ollie what the trouble was.

'The trouble is murder,' Ollie said. 'And arson.'

'I thought you'd already arrested Charlie Harrod's killers.'

'That's right,' Ollie said. 'But let's talk about it at the station house, okay? Some of your friends'll be there, we'll have a regular afternoon tea party.'

Hemmings shrugged, and Ollie followed him inside, gun leveled at him, while he rolled down his sleeves, buttoned his collar, and put on a tie and jacket. By the time they came out into the hallway again, the locksmith had disappeared.

'He didn't fix the lock,' Hemmings said conversationally.

'You don't have to worry,' Ollie said. 'Where you're going, they got plenty of locks.'

Ollie was playing it very big. They already had enough on Hemmings to charge him with Keeping a Disorderly House and possibly with Living on the Proceeds of Prostitution (though here he would most likely claim that even though he was living with a prostitute, he had *other* means of support – his interest in Diamondback Development, for example). But both these offenses were only misdemeanors, and the cops had decided before embarking on their roundup that they were going for broke. By the time Ollie arrested Hemmings, a peculiar internal metamorphosis had taken place; he had begun believing they already had enough on this whole phony bullshit Diamondback Development operation to charge its partners with arson and homicide.

Hawes fell victim to the same euphoric sense of certainty when he arrested Robinson Worthy. The telephone book listed Worthy's address as 198 North Twenty-seventh Street, and that was where he found him at ten minutes past six. Worthy was shaving. He came to the door wearing trousers and an undershirt, his face covered with lather. Hawes was holding a gun in his hand. Worthy said, 'What's that for?'

'We want to ask you a few questions downtown,' Hawes said.

'You don't need the gun,' Worthy said.

'I know I don't. We've got enough without it.'

'Can I finish shaving?'

'Nope,' Hawes said. 'Just wipe it off.'

By the time Roger Grimm arrived at the squadroom, Hawes and Ollie were both riding so high you would have thought the DA had already brought in multiple convictions. Grimm stopped at the slatted railing, looked into the room, saw the detectives sitting at a desk with Worthy and Hemmings, and said, 'All right to come in?'

'Please do,' Hawes said. 'Glad you could come over, Mr Grimm.'

He went to the railing, opened the gate for Grimm, and led him in. Grimm had been called earlier and asked if he could come to the squadroom on a matter pertinent to his arson case. He had, of course, readily agreed to be there at the appointed hour. He did not yet know that *he* was suspected of some high-handed double-dealing with Chase. Had he known, he might have been as apprehensive as Worthy and Hemmings looked. The reason for *their* nervousness was quite simple. The totally unfounded and somewhat giddy confidence emanating from Ollie and Hawes had completely unsettled the Diamondback partners.

'Ollie,' Hawes said, 'this is Mr Roger Grimm, the man who had the fires.'

'How do you do?' Ollie said politely, and rose and took Grimm's hand. 'It's a pleasure to meet you, I've heard so much about you.'

'Good things, I hope,' Grimm said, and smiled weakly. The

confidence was beginning to affect him, too. It was as palpable as an electric current racing around the room. If you touched either of these two cops, you could be electrocuted on the spot.

'And these gentlemen are Mr Robinson Worthy and Mr Oscar Hemmings, partners in a venture known as Diamondback Development. Mr Worthy, Mr Hemmings, Mr Grimm,' Hawes said, and smiled pleasantly.

The men looked at each other. Since Worthy and Hemmings were partners of Chase, and since Grimm was also a partner of Chase, it seemed obvious to the cops that the three of them had at least *heard* of each other. But it now also seemed apparent that this was the first time any of them had met face to face. The confrontation seemed to unsettle Worthy and Hemmings even further. Grimm looked a trifle uncertain as he said, 'Pleased to meet you.' Worthy and Hemmings nodded, and Grimm's uncertainty turned to wariness.

'Well, what do you think?' Ollie said. 'Shall we start without Steve?'

They had already decided that the arrival of Chase would be their surprise card, revealed at the last moment, when the stakes were high and the pot was closed. Carella had told them he would be back at seven sharp. They had asked Grimm to be at the squadroom at six forty-five and it was now six-fifty and the game of poker was about to begin. The interrogation that followed was a peculiar one. Ollie and Hawes played the game as if they were holding a pat royal flush, even though they still needed an essential card – Chase. Worthy and Hemmings, frightened by the wild assurance with which the cops were betting and raising, assumed that their own hands were terrible, whereas in fact they weren't too bad at all. Grimm, sitting with a pair of deuces, watched the proceedings like an out-of-town hick who had been sucked into the game without realizing the stakes were high and the company fast. It was all very peculiar.

'Okay, Mr Worthy,' Ollie said, 'you want to tell us why you spent time with Frank Reardon?'

'I don't know anyone named Frank Reardon,' Worthy said.

This was good for the cops. He was starting with a bluff.

'That's not true,' Hawes said. 'You visited Frank Reardon

several times in the company of Charlie Harrod.'

'Who says so?'

'We have positive identifications from a woman named Barbara Loomis, who's the super's wife in Reardon's building.'

'Well,' Worthy said, and shrugged.

'Were you there to see him, or weren't you?'

'Yes, I was there. That doesn't mean anything.'

'It means you went to visit a person who was employed as a watchman in Mr Grimm's warehouse,' Hawes said. 'Isn't that right, Mr Grimm?'

'That's right,' Grimm said. He looked puzzled, as though trying to determine whether or not his deuces were worth betting.

'Well, Frank Reardon was a friend of mine,' Worthy said.

'Did you know he worked for Mr Grimm?'

'No.'

'I thought he was a friend of yours,' Ollie said.

'Yes, but I didn't know where he was employed.'

'Do you know what Frank Reardon did on August seventh?'

'No,' Worthy said. 'What did he do?'

'Do *you* know what he did, Mr Hemmings?'

Hemmings lighted a cigarette before answering. Then he blew out a stream of smoke and said, 'I don't know Frank Reardon, and I'm sure no one can testify that I ever visited him.'

'That's right,' Ollie said. 'You're absolutely right. No one ever saw you there. All we know is that Harrod, and Mr Worthy here, went to see Frank Reardon. But neither of you know what Reardon did on August seventh, is that correct?'

'That's correct,' Worthy said.

Hemmings nodded and drew in on his cigarette again.

'On that day,' Hawes said, 'Frank Reardon put an unspecified amount of chloral hydrate into a bottle of whiskey.'

'He was paid five thousand bucks to do that,' Ollie said. 'He was paid on August second.'

'He was later shot to death with a Smith & Wesson 9-mm Automatic owned by Charlie Harrod,' Hawes said.

'Is that true? Grimm asked, surprised.

'Yes, that's true,' Hawes said.

'Then you *know* who killed Frank?'

'Yes, Mr Grimm, we know who killed him.' Hawes did not bother to explain that they only knew whose *gun* had killed him. This was no time for playing according to Hoyle, not when so many chips were on the table.

'Then you must also know . . .'

'Patience, Mr Grimm, patience,' Hawes said.

'But *why* was he killed?' Grimm persisted. His deuces were beginning to look good again. He was even contemplating raising the pot a trifle.

'Because he knew exactly how your night watchmen were put out of action,' Hawes said.

'Isn't that right, Mr Worthy?' Ollie said.

Worthy did not answer. He had decided to stand pat with an eight-high diamond flush.

'Mr Hemmings is beginning to feel neglected,' Hawes said.

'We're coming to you, Mr Hemmings,' Ollie said. '*And* your whorehouses. *And* your high-priced little bimbo, Rosalie Waggener. *And* her trip to Germany.'

'*What* trip to Germany?' Hemmings said, calling and raising. He had a full house, aces up, and he was betting the cops did not hold the case ace that would complete their royal flush.

'Oh, didn't you know about that?' Ollie said. 'Gee, didn't she tell you about that? About her trip to Bremerhaven? About taking $500,000 to Bremerhaven?'

Worthy and Hemmings had looked at their cards the moment Ollie had mentioned Bremerhaven, and immediately began studying the huge pile of chips, when they heard about the $500,000 delivered there. Roger Grimm, on the other hand, had begun to go pale the moment he heard Rosalie Waggener's name. He now looked positively ill. He was a man suddenly realizing that a pair of deuces wasn't worth a rat's ass in this kind of poker game. Hemmings was the first to regain his cool. His full house might still be good; recklessly, he raised again.

'Rosalie's never been to Germany in her life,' Hemmings said.

'She went to Germany on July twenty-fifth,' Hawes said.

'We've seen her passport, and she's already told us where she went.'

'To *where*, did you say?'

'To Bremerhaven.'

'Why would Rosalie have gone to Bremerhaven?' Hemmings asked, raising again.

'To deliver that $500,000 to a man named Erhard Bachmann,' Hawes said.

'Know him, Mr Grimm?' Ollie asked.

'Yes, I . . . yes. He's my packer. He packs my . . . my wooden things.'

'How about you, Mr Hemmings? Know anybody named Erhard Bachmann?'

'No,' Hemmings said.

'Mr Worthy?'

'No.'

'Only one here who knows Bachmann seems to be you, Mr Grimm. Do you also know Rosalie Waggener?'

'No,' Grimm said.

Ollie glanced at the clock. It was three minutes to seven.

'Why do you suppose she gave $500,000 to *your* packer?'

'I have no idea,' Grimm said.

'*You* didn't send her to Germany, did you?'

'Me?' Grimm said. 'Me?'

'Did you?'

'Of course not. I don't even know her. How could I . . . ?'

'Oh, that's right,' Hawes said. 'You couldn't have sent her to Germany.'

'That's right,' Grimm said.

'Because Alfie did.'

'Alfie?' Hemmings said, and leaned forward.

'Alfred Allen Chase,' Ollie said. 'Your partner.'

'What!' Hemmings said.

'Shut up, Oscar,' Worthy said.

'Alfie gave the money to Rosalie,' Hawes said.

'To take to Bachmann,' Ollie said.

'You didn't know that, huh, fellows?'

'No,' Worthy said.

'No,' Hemmings said.

'Did *you* know it, Mr Grimm?'

'No,' Grimm said.

'But you *do* know Alfie Chase, don't you?'

'How would I know Alfie Chase?'

'Maybe because you met him in prison,' Hawes said.

'In Castleview,' Ollie said.

'Maybe because you wrote to each other all the time.'

'Maybe because you worked out a little deal together.'

Worthy, Hemmings, and Grimm looked at each other again. Grimm was beginning to realize that his partner, Alfred Allen Chase, had undoubtedly known about the impending warehouse fire and had not warned him. Worthy and Hemmings were beginning to realize that *their* partner, Alfred Allen Chase, had been involved in a side deal with Grimm. The cops did not as yet know what that side deal was, but Hemmings and Worthy knew, and the knowledge wasn't sitting too well with them, judging from the scowls on their faces. It was at this moment that Steve Carella walked into the squadroom with Chase himself. Chase took one look at his multiple assembled partners and seemed ready to bolt for the door.

'This won't hurt but a minute,' Carella said behind him, and nudged him toward the desk.

'Everybody know everybody?' Ollie said. 'Steve, this is Mr Worthy and Mr Hemmings, and I believe you know Mr Grimm. Gentlemen, Detective Steve Carella. And, of course, you all know Alfie Chase because he's your partner.'

'*Everybody*'s partner,' Hawes said.

'You son of a bitch!' Hemmings said, and leaped from his chair, and reached for Chase's throat. His outburst served as the signal for the two other men to spring into action. Worthy came at Chase with a bunched fist, and Grimm simultaneously kicked him in the shin. It was only with some difficulty that the detectives rescued Chase from what might have turned out to be the first squadroom lynching in the history of the Police Department. Ollie slammed Chase down into a swivel chair behind the desk and said, 'What's it all about, Alfie?' which Carella and Hawes thought highly comical, but nobody else even smiled.

The poker game was finished. It was now time to count the chips and turn them in for money – which was, after all, the name of the game.

*

They questioned Alfred Allen Chase alone in the lieutenant's office. They told him many truths and many lies. They started off with a lie.

Q: According to your partners, you're the real heavy in this thing, Alfie. You're the one who told Charlie Harrod to burn down Grimm's warehouse, you're the one who . . .

A: That's a lie.

Q: Charlie wasn't working on your instructions?

A: No. It was their idea. Robbie and Oscar. They're the ones who got Charlie to do the job.

Q: To burn down Grimm's warehouse?

A: Yeah, and his house, too.

Q: Why?

A: Because they found out about him.

Q: About the Bremerhaven deal, do you mean?

A: Yeah.

Q: About the deal with Bachmann?

A: Yeah. They really spilled everything, didn't they? Some partners.

Q: You want to tell us *your* side of it?

A: My side of what?

Q: The deal with Bachmann.

A: Go ask Grimm.

Q: We've already asked him. We want your side of the story.

A: What'd the stupid bastard tell you?

Q: What makes you think he's stupid?

A: Because he's stupid, that's why.

Q: *You're* the one who burned him out, how does that make *him* stupid?

A: *I* didn't burn him out, *they* did.

Q: Why'd they do it, Alfie?

184

A: I told you. They found out about the deal, and they figured the only way to scare him off was to burn down first his warehouse and then his house. Any other time, they might have let him get away with it, but not now when the market's so tight.

Q: When did they find out?

A: The end of July.

Q: Who told them? Bachmann?

A: No, why the hell would he? He had his deal, he had his money, he was happy.

Q: Then who told them?

A: Some fink they know in Germany. He put a call through to Robbie, figured he'd do Robbie a favor, get one back from him later.

Q: Told him that Grimm was dealing with Bachmann, is that right?

A: Yeah.

Q: What kind of deal was it, Alfie?

A: I thought you knew already.

Q: No. What was it?

A: Go find out. I thought they already told you. What the hell is this?

Q: We've got a call in to the Bremerhaven police, they're going to search the cargo and get back to us. You might as well tell us.

A: (Silence)

Q: What do you say, Alfie?

A: The contract is in Grimm's name. For having the animals packed. He's the one you should hang this on. The contract's your proof.

Q: You had nothing to do with it, is that what you're saying?

A: Nothing at all. Nothing with the Bachmann deal, nothing with the fires. I'm clean. *Grimm* was doing business with Bachmann, not me.

Q: How'd Grimm happen to know him?

A: Well, Diamondback did a little business with him before.

Q: With Bachmann?

A: Yes.

Q: When?

A: About six months ago. I had nothing to do with that deal, either. It was all Robbie and Oscar.

Q: What kind of a deal was it?

A: Penny-ante, hardly worth bothering with. We netted two million three.

Q: We?

A: The company. We put eight hundred grand in the bank and split the rest three ways.

Q: In a safety deposit box?

A: The eight hundred? Yeah. They told you that, too, huh? Jesus!

Q: And the rest you split three ways?

A: Yeah. But I didn't know where the money came from. I was clean then, and I'm clean now. I thought it was company profits.

Q: And your share was five hundred thousand?

A: That's right.

Q: Why'd Diamondback keep the eight hundred thousand in reserve? For future deals with Bachmann?

A: I suppose so. But I didn't know anything about what the company planned. I thought it was a legitimate development company. Those guys are trying to put everything on me, when all along *they're* the ones who're maybe involved in some criminal activity. Man, I've been in jail before, you don't think I'd get involved in anything illegal, do you?

Q: You weren't involved in *any* of these deals with Bachmann, is that it?

A: That's *exactly* it.

Q: Not even Grimm's deal.

A: Right.

Q: Then why'd you send Rosalie Waggener to Germany?

A: Who told you that?

Q: Rosalie.

A: Said *I* sent her to Germany?

Q: That's right.

A: She's out of her mind.

Q: She said you gave her five hundred thousand dollars to deliver to Erhard Bachmann.

A: Oh.

Q: Did you?

A: Yeah, but that was a favor to Grimm. He needed somebody to take the money over for him, so I suggested Rosalie. I mean, we knew each other from prison. I figured I'd do him a favor.

Q: That's not what Rosalie told us. Rosalie said it was your money.

A: Well, how would *she* know whose money it was?

Q: She said you were going to make millions.

A: Well, I don't know where she got that idea.

Q: You're not leveling with us, Alfie.

A: I'm telling you the truth.

Q: No, you're *not* telling us the truth. The truth is you were Grimm's partner in the deal.

A: Who told you that?

Q: Grimm.

A: That stupid bastard.

Q: Equal partners. Five hundred thousand each. Come on, Alfie. We know all about it.

A: (Silence)

Q: What do you say?

A: Can't trust a goddamn soul. Boy, oh boy.

Q: *Were* you partners with Grimm?

A: Yeah, yeah.

Q: And it *was* your money Rosalie took to Germany?

A: Yeah.

Q: Why'd you risk sending her?

A: Nobody knew her there. She was using a phony name, there was no way she could be traced back to me. Besides, who was I *supposed* to send? That stupid bastard Grimm? Who let everybody over there tip to him in the first place?

Q: How'd he do that?

A: He told me he needed a cover, he needed to make it all look legit. Protection, he told me. So he actually signed a *contract* for having those wooden animals packed, would you believe it? And he used his right name on it!

Q: What's so special about those animals, Alfie?

A: Nothing.

Q: The Bremerhaven police are right this minute . . .

A: What do I care? Grimm signed the contract, not me.

Q: You just admitted you were partners.

A: That's right, but I didn't know what kind of business he was doing over there.

Q: What kind of business *was* he doing?

A: I wasn't involved in it.

Q: Nobody's saying you were. What was it?

A: There's half a million dollars' worth of heroin inside those animals.

Q: The animals are hollow?

A: Not the other ones Grimm shipped in, but these, yeah. He had them hollowed out, and the dope put inside. The bottoms are plugged.

Q: Then Bachmann's a dealer, right?

A: A merchant.

Q: And what you did was go to Grimm with a source for dope . . .

A: No, no.

Q: . . . knowing he had a way of bringing it in . . .

A: No, you got it all wrong. I was a businessman making an investment. I didn't know what Grimm was involved in.

Q: You're full of shit, Alfie.

A: (Silence)

Q: Alfie?

A: All right, I was trying to make a little money for myself, what the hell's wrong with that? You know how much that scag would've been worth after it was cut? Eleven million dollars! And Jesus, what a sweet setup! I knew where to get the stuff, and Grimm already had a tested way of bringing it in. Every customs official on the dock knew he was running a legit operation, they never so much as glanced at that wooden crap he was importing. Hollow out the animals, stuff them with dope, plug them up again, and we're home free. Perfect. We used to dream of a setup like that when we were in jail together.

Q: But your partners found out about Grimm, and you decided it was safer to sacrifice him than to . . .

188

A: Sacrifice him? He was a stupid bastard. It was *his* fault they found out.

Q: But you couldn't risk their finding out it was *you* who'd double-crossed them in the first place.

A: I *didn't* double-cross them. This was business, pure and simple. A two-way split is better than a three-way split any day of the week.

Q: You're just an enterprising businessman, is that right, Alfie? First you double-cross *one* set of partners, and then you throw your *next* partner to the wolves.

A: What'd you expect me to do? You think Robbie and Oscar were kidding around? Getting Charlie to burn down the warehouse was the first warning. The house in Logan . . .

Q: Why'd Elizabeth Benjamin spend two nights with Reardon?

A: Because he was getting cold feet. They'd already given him five grand, but all of a sudden he was running scared. Liz went over with a little female persuasion.

Q: And the house in Logan?

A: That was the second warning. If Grimm had still tried to bring that shipment in, they'd have had him killed. The way they had Reardon killed after the fire.

Q: Did Charlie take care of that, too?

A: Charlie would've shoved his own mother off the roof for a nickel. He was a junkie, man. He needed lots of loot to keep that habit of his going.

Q: Didn't he make enough with his pornography business?

A: Where'd you guys *get* all this stuff?

Q: Didn't he?'

A: He *used* to. But nowadays you can buy porn right in the open, so what's so special about it? Charlie was on the skids, the Caddy was four years old, the threads were out of style. They supplied him with junk, and he did what they told him to do. In case you haven't heard, the supply's a little short these days. Which is why this would've been such a sweet deal if it wasn't for that stupid bastard Grimm. Why'd he go to *you* guys, would you tell me that? Dumb, that's why. He's involved in an eleven-million-dollar dope deal, so he runs to the cops for help.

Q: He wouldn't have run to us if you hadn't burned down his warehouse.

A: I keep telling you *I* didn't burn it down, *they* did. Send him back to jail, will you? You've got the contract, that's all you need. Send him away for a million years. He's a menace to society.

Q: But not you, huh, Alfie?

A: I was only in it for the bread. You're the ones who taught me, man.

*

At a quarter past nine Rosalie Waggener asked if it was all right if she went home. The detectives told her it was not all right. The detectives told her that they were charging Hemmings, Worthy, and Chase with arson and homicide, and Grimm, Chase, and herself with attempting to smuggle dope into the country.

'I had nothing to do with any dope,' Rosalie said.

'You paid for it,' Carella said.

'I was only a messenger.'

'For a jig pusher,' Ollie said.

'Knock off that kind of talk, will you?' Carella said.

'What kind of talk?'

'That bigoted bullshit,' Hawes said.

'Bigoted?' Ollie said. 'White or black, they're all the same to me, they *all* stink. That's bigoted?'

'That's not even equal but separate,' Carella said, and Ollie burst out laughing. He slapped Hawes and Carella on their backs, simultaneously, with both beefy hands, almost knocking over Carella, who was off balance to begin with. 'I like you guys,' he said, 'you know that? I really enjoy working with you guys.'

Carella and Hawes said nothing. Since Ollie had just confessed to a monumental misanthropic outlook, Carella was wondering why he had now bestowed upon them the singular honor of his affection. Hawes, on the other hand, was wondering what mistake he'd made. Had he somehow indicated to

190

Ollie that he'd *wanted* his friendship? Jesus, had he unwittingly done *that*?

'You know what I think I'm gonna do?' Ollie said. 'I think I'm gonna put in for a transfer to the 87th. I really do *like* you guys.'

Again Carella and Hawes said nothing. Hawes was thinking they already *had* an Ollie Weeks up at the old station house, and his name was Andy Parker, and if Ollie transferred to the 87th, Hawes would immediately ask for a transfer to the 83rd. Carella was thinking that Ollie's addition to the squad would create a fine kettle of fish – Ollie himself, another jewel named Andy Parker, a black cop named Arthur Brown, and a Puerto Rican cop named Alexiandre Delgado. The potential mix was pregnant, so to speak. Carella shuddered at the thought.

'Is it all right to go to the ladies'?' Rosalie asked.

*

In bed that night, Carella had trouble falling asleep. He kept thinking of Alfred Allen Chase's last words in the Q and A.

'You're the ones who taught me, man.'

It was not that he hadn't understood what Alfie had meant, or exactly whom he was indicting. It was merely that as a white man, he had enormous difficulty *accepting* Alfie's indictment.

When he finally did fall asleep, he tossed and turned a lot, and his dreams were bad.

Ed McBain
Blood Relatives 60p

Saturday night, and party night on the Precinct – the
perfect backdrop for a knife-carrying sex attacker.
Seventeen year-old Muriel was stabbed to death and her
cousin Patricia got away with a slashed cheek. When she
ran into the station house Kling watched the bloody
hand-prints appear on the glass panel. A messy start to a
case that got messier – every time Patricia changed her
story . . .

He Who Hesitates 50p

Roger didn't want a uniformed cop, he wanted a detective.
He met Detective Parker, and Parker was the son of a
bitch. How could he tell a man like that about going to
bed with Molly – and not getting excited – and everything?
Head down against the snow, Roger began to follow
Detective Steve Carella . . .

'Gripping all the way . . . ' IRISH TIMES

Hail to the Chief 50p

Carella looked into the frozen ditch as Kling fanned his
flashlight over the naked bodies. Who was responsible?
The Death's Heads, the Scarlet Avengers or the Yankee
Rebels? A couple of detectives with six corpses on their
hands needed all the help they could get, and they
wouldn't get it from the gangs, that was sure . . .